Volume 17

A Vita Unwin Mystery

G. K. HOLCOMB

ScrutableBooks

Athens, Ohio

Go to ScrutableBooks.com

ISBN: 0991288009
ISBN-13: 978-0991288007

To two lovers of the mystery:
Toby "Tessie" Rachel (née Brownson) Holcomb (in memoriam);
and Annette "Nicki" (née Nicas) Mahnke.

PART I

1

Okay. This is what happened.

The leg between LAX and Paris was late, very late. Feeling what my mother used to call "owly" after the overnighter—that feeling that your eyes are wide open but everything behind them is coated with dust—I grabbed my carryon and ran to the gate, barely made it, out of breath and looking my usual disheveled self. Complete with puffy hair, smeared lipstick, and perspiration drips. Not even a spare moment to check myself in a mirror till I took my seat. Then, an attempt to put the frizzy mass back into some kind of order, to dab the undereyes and fix the lipstick.

It would be a short hop to Bucharest at least. Then the hotel and sleep and a long bath and finally food and drink.

The plane taxied and then sat there, a staticky voice announcing some delay, a plane loading at the gate. Even in business class, my knees almost touched the seat in front of me, and I rearranged my legs for the umpteenth time. I turned to the passenger next to me to commiserate about the delay, but the woman turned away brusquely, as if intentionally, and peered deeply into some sort of serious-looking book.

I opened my laptop and felt a pang of envy. I hate—almost hate—those people who can travel and still look like that. Makeup and hair smooth and untroubled. Clothes seemingly just pressed. Did other people have some magic I lack? I do try. I am coiffed by the finest hair stylist I can afford in West L.A. I shop in fine shops in the Beverly Center and have any imperfectly fitting clothes tailored. It doesn't matter. I can, for an hour or two, look good. But then things just naturally degrade until I am a floppy mess once again. Everything returns to its natural state.

I noted the woman's hands, smooth and pale with very fine skin and tapered nails. Except for the striking-looking scar on her right hand, a nasty slash diagonally across the veins.

Sitting there in the plane, immobile on the tarmac, a series of involuntary thoughts came to me. Memories of *Ion*, of my time in Romania so many years ago.

I'd met Ion at that Bucharest hotel reception. Or *seen* Ion, that is, first. And this is how I remembered it.

He was surrounded by a small crowd of admirers, spinning hilariously about the Dictator's bizarre conduct and the buffoonish ways of his family. Everyone gazed up at him—he was even taller than I am—amused but intent.

"He's made a scepter for himself—you know, an old emperor's sword!" he managed to get out between spasms of hysterics. His laughter sparked off a round of mirth. "And he calls himself 'The Genius of the Carpathians'!" He had to lay a hand on the shoulder of a man to catch his breath, but continued. "He demands that his illiterate wife be made a member of the American Academy of Sciences *and* the British Royal Institute of Chemistry! And all Romanian scientists have to cite her in their research! He says his thick son is a nuclear physicist!

"He wanted to make a national hero of Vlad the Impaler," he went on, "the medieval ruler the rest of the world knows as 'Dracula.' This was because in his mind the Americans, with their weird pop culture fixation with Dracula, think that Romanians are evil. He hit on a brilliant idea of how to turn the tables on the supposed American demonization of Romanians on account of Dracula. He would name himself the modern incarnation of Vlad! But, you know, Vlad Țepeș committed unspeakable crimes even against his people. So the idea of digging him up and making a hero out of him sank like a Romanian sub!"

He was fearless. Saying these things at the time would have jeopardized his life. The Dictator's enforcers—along with blackmailers and informers, spies and conspirators, money launderers and financial opportunists, and various plants and characters of every stripe—crammed the hotel. It was a kind of darker version of Rick's Place in *Casablanca*. It was difficult to know whom to trust.

And then in one of those corny seeing-each-other-across-a-crowded-room scenes, we'd locked eyes. When he winked at me, I realized I'd been staring at him. I gave him a crooked smile, blinked, shook the dust out of my head, watched as he left the group he'd been talking to and came toward me.

When Ion stood in front of me, only inches away, I felt an instantaneous chemical reaction, an irresistible pull. Chemistry. *And all Romanian scientists would have to acknowledge it.* I'd never felt it before. I'd always thought the idea was silly. But now there it was, simply there. I felt his attraction toward me. He seemed to work to hold his eyes up to my own, rather than let them wander around and up and down my body. That would come later.

He laughed when he told me his name was pronounced *Yawn*. The last thing I thought of when I thought about Ion.

"You're a writer," he said, looking at me, his smile verging on immodesty. "But a special kind. You don't write the usual thing. Like I do. I'm a common journalist. You do something quite different."

I stared back at him, wondering how he knew this about me.

"No, I'm nothing. I'm just a girl. I like to eat new things and write about them, and hope I don't get sick from eating them."

He let out an uproarious laugh. "Perfect!" he said. "Perfect!"

He'd asked me my preference, and brought me a fresh drink.

We moved on to a quieter area, just naturally started talking, asking each other questions, leaning in close ostensibly to hear better, but really to be physically near. At that first meeting Ion didn't tell me much about his life. Only that he'd been a journalist, but cautiously suggesting that there was more to it, something he didn't reveal easily. The revelations and truths would come out later, whispered, heads on pillows. I would learn the origins of those lines that made his otherwise young face appear so careworn.

I'd gone to Romania on a US government grant, one that would pay me to be an "independent researcher," enough to survive and a little more. My dim apartment was provided, and living and traveling were cheap, and I would have time to work on my first book. I was beginning to make a modest living for myself as a freelance writer about food, culture, art, travel. I existed mostly on the margins, though, scraping up just enough money to live in the States while aggressively competing for travel writing jobs. I knew this would be the only way I could afford to see the big old world, for a while.

Ion and I talked about people who didn't want to go anywhere.

"How could you want to just stay in one place!" I said. "You'd watch your life spinning away season to season, year to year.

"I started collecting maps and globes when I was a kid." I'd never talked about this with a stranger before. "I liked action stories, with pirates and sailors and gunslingers, and stories about real people who did things, like fly planes and climb mountains. And I liked stories from far off places about genies and banshees."

Most men interrupt girls, as if they needed to be told what they think. He'd listened, looking at me with intensity. "You're an adventurer. The last of the old gang. You belong in the romantic past, when lusty men and women seized their world."

Though I was certain that he knew *lusty* didn't mean lustful, I nevertheless blushed at the word. As if he'd read my thoughts.

"My parents didn't try to make me more girlish," I told him. "They fed my interests as well as they could and watched with some bemusement, as if scratching their heads. 'Where did this strange creature come from?' And now, here I am writing about food, such a woman's milieu."

"But food and travel. Food and culture. Food and adventure," Ion had clarified for my imagined, future critics.

I'd fallen in love with him that same night, in this order—the order in which I'd encountered him—face, body, voice, and then his whole self, his mind and character.

I felt ridiculously swoony around him, loved his thick brown hair and dark piercing eyes. He wore clothes well, as if every item was tailored just for him.

Another thing that pulled me to him was his past, as I learned of it little by little, his suffering at the hands of the Dictator's "enforcers." Just bullies, and thugs with power. He'd been a voice of reason, a critic of the regime, a journalist with a potent pen. He'd investigated and written about government corruption, about ridiculous riches among the political elite, about starving peasants and urban squalor. He wrote for international markets, his work censored in his home country, and for little pay. He'd used a different, professional name for writing, to protect himself from detection.

For the first couple of years after I'd left the country, we'd written letters back and forth, always with a plan to meet up somewhere in the world. Then it was email. While I continued to see other men, I was hopeful we would get back together.

Then all messages from Ion stopped, and after the usual bout of self-doubt and heartbreak, I pushed Ion to the back of my mind and went on with my life, which consisted of professional successes and personal disappointments.

Suddenly about a year ago Ion sent me a message and we began corresponding again. He'd married, had a son who was now grown, and had gotten divorced, the usual modern story. Now that he was free, he desperately wanted to see me. He had for years, but believed in the contract of marriage.

During the year that Ion and I started up again, my most recent book was published in Romanian, and I was invited by the State Department to visit Romania and give a few talks. It was meant to be.

I wondered how it would go, you know, whether it was ever possible to retrieve the past or whether it would disappoint. Whether I'd find out the past was a lie.

"Ridiculous to worry about things you can't change," I scolded myself. "The future will take care of itself."

2

After I'd passed through customs, and the brief interview with the surly customs officer, I saw the sign: "Vita Unwin." Even I started at the improbability of my name emblazoned across a large white sign in dark red letters.

The young man holding the sign was waiting at the baggage claim. The Consulate had sent him to be my driver and liaison. He was a handsome young man named Radu, dark haired, dark complected, dark eyed. He gazed up at me.

"It's wonderful to meet you, Ms. Unwin!" Radu said, beaming. "I'm very happy you have come."

"I'm happy to have come, myself."

Just out the airport's doors, taxi drivers stepped into our way, but Radu only politely declined, sidestepping the men. In the parking lot, several aggressive young men and boys shadowed us, one of them even shoving aside a smaller boy while a bigger one tried to grab my suitcase from Radu's hand. Was it a staged fracas, a diversion so that an accomplice could snatch a suitcase? Or were they merely fighting over who would have the chance to carry the bags and receive a somewhat extorted tip?

Radu just held onto the bags, making sure I was in front of him, and made his way quickly to the car, an old Dacia beater.

He effortlessly hefted my large suitcase and stowed it in the trunk of the car, and then directed me to the backseat, holding the door and only smiling when I suggested sitting up front with him. "Please, madam," he said, with such a bright, disarming smile that I practically melted into the thick leather seat.

Radu asked me how my flight had been.

"I feel like I'm going to fall into a coma! But I'll be recovered in a few days. I'm very excited about being back in Romania!" I laughed, and Radu seemed to start a little.

I was sitting in back, but spent the drive leaning forward, getting as close to the front as the seatbelt would allow, asking Radu about himself. I assumed he'd already been told about me.

"I do odd jobs for the Consulate to pay for school and the apartment I share with two other students," he said. "I drive, help with office moves, squire important people around, translate when needed." I wasn't surprised that he knew several languages. Romanians are able linguists. No doubt due to millennia of foreign occupation—Romans, Turks, Germans,

Hungarians, Russians.

"And I'll be joining you on your book tour," he added.

I had been given to understand that a translator would be assigned to me for the tour, but hadn't been provided any details about who the person would be.

"Oh, that is delightful! We can get to know each other."

While he talked, his story being so familiar to me, I could not stop the rush of memories. In my mind Bucharest was always dim and misty, crawling with intrigue and dark secrets. But today the dazzling sun nearly turned even the Soviet style apartment towers a gleaming, startling white. Recent rains had cleaned the cars and storefronts and streets. Everything shone. I felt somehow disappointed, and scoured the passing streets for signs of my remembered city.

"I got a copy of your book. I have a copy in translation." He held up my book, *Snouts, Tails, Entrails: The Story of Offal*, translated into Romanian, his other hand on the steering wheel. I looked at the title in Romanian, stupefied by the sight of it. "I look forward to reading it," he continued. "It has such an intriguing title."

"It's great that it's finally been translated into Romanian. And I'm interested in hearing what Romanians think of it." I paused, choosing my words, not wanting to slight the translation. "But I'd like to give you an English copy. I'm sure the translation is first-rate, but you know what the poet says gets lost in the translation."

"Frost said it was *the poetry*," Radu said, and I could see he was happy with his display of erudition.

As we passed University Square, Radu talked about this being the site of student protests, speaking in the natural English foreigners can only get through American music, movies, and TV. "The army fired into the crowds, killing so many." He went on about the revolution. I already knew all this, but didn't interrupt.

Then he pointed out the university, and a former party restaurant that no longer drew the elite, as it was white-tableclothed and considered stodgy. The young, as all young, hung out in trendier—that is to say, cheaper—places.

Distant but unmentioned sat the scathingly named People's Palace, a vast, squat monstrosity overlooking all, a megalomaniac's dream of a power greater than that housed in the Pentagon.

We passed elegant storefronts, behind which were displayed expensive-looking clothes. I noted more, and more varied, cars on the streets, more signs, more colors, home décor shops, people in snazzy getups alongside Gypsies and the black-clad babushkas of the old world.

The dogs. The dogs were still there. Countless smart stray dogs. Dogs that waited to cross the streets until the lights changed and they were accompanied by a human. People fed them, I'd learned on my past visit. The Romanians liked, some even loved, the roaming dogs. Romanians cared for and all but adopted some street dogs. Dogs belonged to certain apartment buildings or streets where people fed them.

"Things have changed a lot since I lived here. There weren't any stores like this." I remembered the glum shopping of the past, with floor upon floor of the same cheap merchandise, and the stout, disagreeable women who served.

"And the only cars I saw were the Romanian Dacias." I thought about it for a moment, realizing I was riding in a fairly aged Dacia. "Like this one, only boxier." I indicated Radu's sedan. "But we didn't really see a lot of cars on the streets, back then."

"It was very bleak then. Some things have improved."

"And what about the government? My impression's that some things changed under the new order, but a lot stayed the same."

I waited, and then he spoke, apparently choosing his words: "People say that the corruption now is as bad as it was under the communists, maybe worse. People say that at least before the revolution, everyone had a job and could eat."

While Radu was talking, we were waiting at a traffic light, and I watched an extended family of Gypsies, the women and girls in traditional dress, crossing the street. They were dark completed, small, and silent. They were conspicuous among Romanians in stylish outfits and business wear.

"Tell me about the Roma," I said. I used the word I understood they prefer to be called. "Can you tell me whether attitudes toward the Gypsies have improved?" I knew this was a hazardous topic. Before returning to Romania, I'd read a wonderful book by an American woman who'd spent time with Albanian, Polish, Bulgarian, and Romanian Gypsies.

Radu stiffened, as he drove through the traffic, and then laughed. He seemed to change the subject: "Some of us feel that a very important thing we can do now is to preserve the Romanian patrimony. Architecture, art, music, dance, literature—all of the national heritage in need of preservation as things change so fast."

3

Stunted-looking, ragged Gypsy women and their undersized children quietly but persistently begged near the doors of the grand hotel, the splendid old corner building with ornately railed balconies and arched windows. Radu regarded the

Romani beggars silently, and started to walk into the hotel with my bags. But I stopped him, asking him to give them some of my change. And I wanted him to wish them well for me.

Radu looked at me, impassive, then turned toward the women, distributing equally among them the lei, the Romanian currency, I'd handed him. He spoke softly to them, while I stood by, smiling at the women. The women turned to me and thanked me, bobbing their small dark heads.

The tall, broad-shouldered, outlandishly uniformed doorman gazed at Radu.

"That wasn't Romanian, was it?"

Radu paused. "It was Romani, their language."

"Well, you do know a lot of languages!"

"We Romanians are known for being linguists. I have studied several languages."

"So you're my personal linguist. Very practical."

I was sure that when I had been in Romania the first time, I didn't know a Romanian who knew the Romani language. With the possible exception of Ion, I hadn't met any Romanians who were interested in the Gypsies.

Radu stood by my side while I checked in. The young woman took my passport and checked the computer about my room.

I stood there, taking in the hotel, the place where I'd first met Ion. Soaking it all in, after so many years had passed. I stood on the gray, inlaid marble floor and gazed at the pink marbled pillars and soaring ceilings that seemed somehow to absorb sound.

People coursed through the lobby, workers busy loading luggage onto carts, guides gathering their charges, smartly dressed people lounging on divans and speaking to each other, but all the sound that should have been a cacophony was oddly hushed. Or maybe it was my weariness that dampened the sound.

My room had a superb view of the enormous central city square, with its symphony hall and the national library. But sleep was all I could think about. Radu made arrangements to pick me up the next day and deliver me to the Consulate for my complete itinerary, and in my room I gratefully sank into a luxurious bed thick with white linens.

4

When I roused myself it was dark. My body was completely out of whack. Biorhythms, I guessed. The city outside bustled with night activities. Dance. Music. Drink. Food.

As a food writer, my first travel meal usually filled me with anticipation. What delights to discover! My memory of Romanian cooking was that the home food I'd been fortunate to eat was always delicious, if simple.

However, I was a guest of the country, and had mingled with prominent people who often socialized in restaurants that "the people" couldn't afford to go. And for a city that claimed links to Paris, the restaurant food had been disappointing. The menus were far too long, pages and pages, each condiment listed separately—a parsley garnish, a pat of butter, a piece of bread— each dish à la carte, too many choices, and in the end it didn't matter much what one chose. I usually went for chicken or fish, especially if they had trout—the trout would be fresh from some local river, clean tasting and simply cooked—since it was hard to mess up and not too strange for my young palate.

How odd that now I eat offal! A consumer of unwanted parts.

Because I couldn't read Romanian, I'd had to puzzle my way through the inevitable "English" menu, a kind of surrealist game where the reader must be nearly clairvoyant to understand what was being expressed.

The first time I'd seen a "Plate of Crap," I'd burst out laughing. When I asked what a Plate of Crap was, someone told me it was a *carp* dish.

Time had passed, though, and I imagined many things had passed with it.

Ion again came unasked into my mind, as he often did. He'd just suddenly be there, with his dark eyes, his head bending to mine, his arm lightly but somehow insistently around my waist, his dark laugh.

I was excited. I would see him tomorrow night. We had exchanged emails, talked about the idea of meeting again on my very first night back in Bucharest. But I knew I'd be wrecked that first evening, after fourteen hours of flying, so told him that I would have to force myself to wait and to see him the next night. Tomorrow evening we would meet again, after so long. I felt the anticipation charge through my fatigued body. Pleasure deferred.

Now I had to eat.

I wasn't feeling up for a walk, or a taxi ride, so called down for a table at the hotel's restaurant. When I walked in I was surprised by the amount of light, the sleek tables, and the lack of the damned lacy white tablecloths! The chic wooden chairs, the room divider made, charmingly, of wine corks caught between panes of glass, the sleek bar, the round cubbies for wine bottles. It could have been a restaurant in L.A. or New York or London or Berlin.

The menu was also a wonderful surprise. First, it ran only to two pages. Second, it was interesting, comforting, neither stodgy nor uber-hip, and no "crap" in sight! The wine list was longer than the food menu. It was arranged by country (Romania, France, Italy) and by grape and region. My head just couldn't take it all in at the moment. I was in my typical post-travel fog. Tomorrow I hoped to be as right as rain.

So I asked the waiter to choose a wine for me, and after asking me a couple of questions to gauge my taste, he suggested a Romanian wine called Saturnalia. He said the wine came from the Dealu Mare region, famous for its red wines, and that it was a "Burgund Mare" varietal, a grape I was unfamiliar with. He described the wine as being all about *terroir*, soil, in the French style of a Gamay.

Good man, I thought. He was a neat young fellow who reminded me of the new wave of Parisian servers, smiling, even cheerful, well informed, and unobtrusive.

Even with a reasonable sized menu, it was still hard to choose, especially when one was famished. Hmmm. To start, the pan-fried scallops with pancetta on celeriac puree? Or the paté? House made. Then a simple minestrone with pesto. Or a salad of baby greens and local goat's cheese. For the main, slow-roasted lamb shanks with rosemary potatoes and sautéed spinach on the side. Or the grilled calves' liver. Or maybe I felt more like pappardelle with rabbit ragù.

To end, maybe some cheese, or something chocolate, and of course a cup of strong café crème. I drilled the waiter about each choice for his preference, and finally had a meal ordered. Exhausted from the effort, I sat back with a loud sigh and a weary laugh.

"Well, aren't we glad that's over!"

The waiter did no more than raise his eyebrows almost imperceptibly to indicate that he was impressed by the size of my order, confirmed that my choices were all excellent ones, even though he'd been responsible for the actual choosing, disappeared and returned quickly with my wine.

He performed the ritual of showing me the bottle, and with his sommelier knife opened it cleanly like a pro should, and poured me a taste, waiting for my approval. I took a sip and nearly whooped with delight. It was dusty and layered. I was tasting the very Romanian earth.

The waiter, this consummate professional, could not help himself and grinned widely at my small outburst. "Very good, madam!" Within moments—what was he, a ninja?—he disappeared again and returned with a basket of warm, crusty bread and perfectly chilled butter. Ah, perhaps I was in Paris, after all!

My position at a well-placed table, backed to a side wall, gave me a clear view of the comings and goings of the patrons and servers. My glass seemed magically to fill whenever it got dangerously low, and I remembered how in the other time it was considered a terrible faux pas, and caused much agitation among wait staff and management, to reach for the bottle to refill one's own empty glass.

As I drank the delightful wine and ate thickly buttered pieces of bread, I surveyed the room.

The restaurant was a tower of Babel, all manner of languages being spoken, the people a modern mix of old world elegance and new world hipsterism. I wondered if the hotel was still "crawling with intrigue."

I was sitting in a lovely room with the remains of a delicious meal before me. And it was late, and I was tired again. A night's sleep always restored me to my bright and sanguine self.

My cell phone rang while I lounged in the nice, deep—but as always too short—tub with lots of hot water and bubbles. I stuck out my tongue at the old-fashioned ring tone. Nothing could be worth getting out of the tub for.

The voice that left the message was a deep, soft rumble that had always made me think of Scotch and very dark chocolate. My breath caught. Until now I had only missed Ion in the abstract, as a memory—and how reliable a memory? But hearing his voice made him real to me again.

As I did with writing, food, and other passions, I have always given myself whole, without reservations, to affairs of the heart. I threw myself recklessly into love. I'd had a few—quite a few, actually—love affairs since Ion, but the relationships were short-lived. They either ended in a scene or just trailed off. I wondered at times if I hadn't sabotaged them myself, whether I hadn't just broken attachments because they weren't worth holding together.

A direct man who always knew exactly what he wanted, Ion left his message with no preamble. He'd pick me up at the hotel at seven the next evening.

Instead of falling into bed in my usual jet-lagged stupor, I was suddenly full of useless energy, so stood and stared at my wardrobe. I did best in blacks and grays and browns. I felt that brighter colors made me appear clownish.

I had one slinky dress that really needed to be worn with heels, albeit short ones, and while Ion was taller than I am— remarkable in itself—he wasn't that much taller. I'd rather look him in the eye than tower above him in heels. I also had a little black dress—maybe not so little on my tall frame—one that wrapped around my waist and made me feel comfortable and attractive, and which I could wear flats with. That, with a blue silk scarf.

Hair. I couldn't do much about my hair. I'd gotten it cut just before leaving. Cut and colored. The color looked good, but I struggled getting my hair to do what I wanted. "Oh, who cares,"

I told the critical self looking back at me from the mirror. "Ion wants to see you, you idiot. Not your hair."

Looking in the mirror, I decided that my body hadn't changed much. I have one of those bodies people envy, long and lean, and aside from a few extra but well-distributed pounds, it's essentially the same, year after year. I truly can eat anything I want, so long as I don't start downing calories like a sumo wrestler or an Olympic swimmer, and so long as I do more than sit on my rear all day. Writing days have to have activity in them: walking, running, rowing, swimming, something. I've found that travel actually serves as activity, and am usually down a few pounds after a trip, though when I can I like to get out for a run in a park.

Anticipation makes me restless. The city wasn't the same at it had been back then. Streets were well lit and cars of all kinds dashed everywhere. Horns honked, people spilled out of bars and cafés. Like New York. It wasn't so very late, so I took myself for a walk.

Passing dazzling store windows full of luxury goods that naturally sprang up near the grand hotel, letting my eyes wander and my mind go to the next night, where it wanted to be, I suddenly felt that prickle you feel when you're being watched. I heard footfalls, almost in step with mine.

I stopped. They stopped.

Yes, the streets were full of cars, and the cafés full of revelers, but a woman being followed could never feel completely safe. I stepped inside a hip-looking restaurant, went straight up to the bar, and then let myself look around. Through the window I could see someone, the shadow of someone, standing as if waiting for me. I ordered a glass of wine and nursed it, hoping the pursuer would give up and go away. I told myself I could probably hold my own with anyone who was unarmed. I'm strong, tough, and tall, but why take chances?

Forty-five minutes later I was sick of waiting, and now genuinely weary. Ready for bed. "Oh, eff it," I said to myself. And stormed out, making myself appear as big and blustery and unafraid as I could manage. The hotel was only across the plaza. No one would dare attack me so boldly, on the street, with witnesses all around. Right?

As I began to stride down the street, I heard a quiet voice say, "*Doamnă, doamnă.*" "Lady, lady." Turned and saw a hand held out for alms. The hand belonged to a small, dark-skinned child in bare feet and tattered clothes. The Roma. A Gypsy. *Țigani.* Romani. A Romani child begging, his mother or sister probably nearby, maybe the mother the one whose steps I'd heard.

It was a common sight in the capital, same as in most US cities, especially near the big hotels: poor people begging. The Romani set up there to importune the rich foreign visitors for money, and some, I suppose, set up to rob said rich foreigners. I'd never heard of a Romani person raping or violently attacking any foreigner, though—the reverse, more like. Anyway, it was just money. And I had money.

I berated myself for being scared of a begging child, or maybe the child's mother. Smiled down at him. Gave him about two dollars worth of lei and went back to my room and slept as if I were in a coma.

5

I sat in a mahogany paneled antechamber of the US Consulate, waiting for the cultural attaché, a man I had only encountered through the appearance of his signature on my lecture tour agreement. The man's name was Richard Elbow. The smiling office assistant had asked me to be seated, and I had smiled back, thinking that the attaché must be familiarly known as *Dick Elbow*.

Could the legendary Romanian sculptor of eccentric human forms Anton Cozma have given artistic shape, I mused, to such an anatomical construction? Later this evening, I decided that I would relate this name to Ion. He would appreciate the humor.

While waiting, I read a copy of *The International Herald Tribune*, an article about the treatment of the Romani people in Eastern Europe. The article said that the Roma weren't faring much better under the present government than they had under the previous.

I realized I knew nothing of their food culture, and felt a bit displeased with myself about this fact. I supposed it must be much like Romanian fare, though—the polenta-like dish called *mămăligă*, the meat in aspic, the farmer's cheese, and various other simple country dishes and staples.

Eventually, Dick Elbow came out into the waiting room and greeted me. In his suit and wingtips, he looked like a man who could have walked through the door from nearly any moment in the 20th or even 21st century. He seemed preoccupied, hurrying out of his office, no doubt multitasking, so was not focusing on me as he approached.

I stood up to greet him. He actually stepped back, mouth a little open, as he gazed up at me.

He looked so neat and put together, well combed and shaved. I felt rumpled and frizzled, under the weight of the jet lag and usual afternoon dishabille.

Sitting across from him at his polished, tidy desk I accepted a cup of coffee, and we exchanged preliminary pleasantries. Two copies of my book sat on his desk, both the English original and the new Romanian translation. The diplomat asked how my flight was, and how I was doing.

"I'm on the verge of falling into a coma every half hour!" I said. "But I'll be in the pink in a day or two. I'm thrilled to be back in Romania!" I laughed. I'm told I have a booming laugh.

His eyes momentarily widened.

"That's right," he said, "you've been here before." Of course he knew I'd been to Romania before, as these people like nothing more than collecting information on people, ordinary and celebrated. I see myself as neither. I think of myself as extraordinary and know that I'm not famous.

"Yes, back in the bad old times. I was a restless traveler in my salad days. I still travel, but not with the fortitude I once had."

We sat in silence for a moment. I assumed the file also indicated my connection to the famous Ion Vadim.

And I wondered vaguely whether the file was accurate, and, if so, how they'd found out the things that had been put in it. I felt ambivalent about the fact that the state had collected information on me, both appalled by the invasion of privacy and a little flattered that I drew such interest.

"Were you doing research for one of your food books?" he asked. "Romanian cuisine would make an interesting study."

"Yes, and no," I said. "Really, I was on the bum then. Still relatively young and footloose, a blithe spirit."

"I've been reading your new book. It's very interesting." He flipped through the English copy on his desk. "*Snouts, Tails, Entrails: A Story of Offal*. I'd never thought about food in that way before. I'm curious to see how Romanian audiences respond to it."

I said I was also curious to hear their response. I did not go into how important Romania had been in thinking about the book, the way Romanians had used all parts of the animals they ate. I didn't talk about Romanian food at length in the book, in any case.

Glancing at his watch, Dick Elbow got down to the business of confirming the itinerary they'd sent me.

Radu, the young man who had picked me up at the airport, had volunteered to take me out on the town, to meet some of the younger people, and that would take place tomorrow.

The next day I would be interviewed on a Romanian TV show. It was a show devoted to cultural matters. The show would provide a translator for me. It would be a twenty-minute segment, and rebroadcast while I was on my brief speaking tour.

And the following morning I would begin the first leg of the lecture tour. I would start off with a visit to a city north of Bucharest, famous for its Gothic church, and speak at a mountain resort. Then on to the old Hungarian capital and second most populous city in the country, where I would talk at the Transylvanian national museum. After that, it was on to another Transylvanian city, to lecture at another museum.

My next talk would be back in Bucharest, at the national art gallery, in the salon where a selection of works by the controversial artist Anton Cozma would be exhibited for the first time. The room was to be called the Cozma Cabinet.

The prospect of speaking in the same room as *Last Supper*—a work that had nearly obsessed me for years—thrilled me. I'd read that the special exhibit was coming to Bucharest, so that had become another reason to return to Romania. In fact, I regarded it as something of a deal breaker when I agreed to do the tour. After seeing a digital, three-dimensional rendering of *Last Supper* in Los Angeles, I had decided to write an article about the sculpture. I then had collected all of the published images of it I could find and studied them for many hours.

It was the context. *Last Supper*, I felt, must be witnessed in Romania. I longed to see the sculpture, in person, and to relive the shock and admiration I had felt for it through the reproduced images. Only a few artworks—a triptych by Francis Bacon and one or two others—had affected me in such a way. Whatever it was, *Last Supper* had somehow both frightened and thrilled me. It had felt like a glimpse of something real.

"I would have come back to Romania if only to experience the sculpture," I said. "I've written a special talk just for Bucharest that focuses on it. I have some images I'll show. I hope it's stimulating for a Romanian audience."

Shortly after the talk in Bucharest, I would go on the second part of my tour, traveling to the northeastern part of the country. I would take a train to a city known as Romania's "Cultural Capital," Iaşi.

I smiled at the pronunciation. *Yosh*. I hadn't thought about it in a long time. "You know, when I first came to Romania and saw that word, I pronounced it *Ee*-yaw-*see*. I discovered how direct Romanians could be by the way they corrected me."

"Everyone pronounces it that way at first," Elbow said. "I did."

"It's that little *i* at the end that throws everyone off. Like the artist Brâncuşi. Everyone outside of Romania pronounces it 'Brankoozy.' As if it were kind of an Italian name. *Bronkoosh*," I said.

In Iaşi, I would give a talk at a place called the Palace of Culture, where the likes of Harriet Beecher Stowe had lectured on an international *Uncle Tom's Cabin* book tour.

"Harriet Beecher Stowe, no less!" I said. "'The little woman who wrote the book that started this great war.'" I admired Stowe and the "damned mob of scribbling women."

Elbow wasn't familiar with the latter quotation.

"Oh! Nathanial Hawthorne!" I heard my inner literary nerd saying. "He hated the fact that women writing sentimental books were successful while he struggled to sell his own novels."

After that stop, I would take the train down to Constanţa, on the Black Sea, to talk at a resort there.

"Of course!" I said, continuing in the vein of literary geek. "The city Augustus exiled poor Ovid from Rome to for writing *The Art of Love*."

All of my travel would be done by rail. I hadn't been told this while communicating with the assistant and was a bit surprised. My memory of Romanian train travel was not positive.

I told Elbow about one train ride I'd taken during the winter. The heating system had been located under the bench seats. I had come back from the alleged dining car, sat down on the bench seat, and jumped up, exclaiming a common American epithet.

"It burned my ... behind," I told Dick Elbow. I'd been thinking of another word. "I had to stand for the rest of the trip."

And the cigarette smoking was intolerable. Of course, asking Romanians not to smoke was impossible—they would look at you as if you must be nuts. When I had opened a window for a breath of the bracing cold air, fellow passengers jumped up and slammed the window shut, yelling, "*Curent! Curent!*"—"The draft! The draft!" It was one of the few Romanian words I remembered. Romanians had believed that drafts could cause illnesses. It seemed like most Romanians I met smoked their lungs black but shrieked in panic at the idea of circulating air.

"It must be different now, though," I said.

He'd listened in silence, then reassured me that train travel in Romania had improved since the communist days.

And Radu, the young man who had picked me up at the airport, would be accompanying me.

"Oh, yes!" I said. "Radu told me this when he picked me up. He seems like a very capable young man. At first, I thought he must be an American. His English sounded like he must be from out West somewhere." I thought for a moment. "Colorado." I was satisfied that my deduction was quite precise.

"Radu is an up-and-coming young scholar of Romanian culture," said Elbow. "His interest is in preserving the country's patrimony."

Patrimony, I thought. Yes, I remembered him talking about this in the car. It wasn't a word one would hear being used in the States. *National heritage?* I frankly didn't like the sound of it.

6

The next day I was glad for the distractions that kept me from clock-watching. There was so much crap to do, little arrangements to make, but then it all led to seven.

And then there he was, sitting in the lobby, long legs easily, elegantly crossed. As he rose I noted that he looked almost exactly as I'd remembered, except with deeper lines in his face and graying hair. Still dashing. Still electric.

We didn't speak. He put his arms around me, kissed my hair, and I almost suggested we just skip the "date" and get right to business. But, pleasure deferred is even greater pleasure, right?

"Vita." He murmured my name several times.

"How are you, Ion?" I asked, barely able to contain myself. "You look well."

"I'm well now," he said. "I've been waiting for you to come back. It's been too long. I almost forgot what it felt like."

He stepped back and looked at me. "You look the same!"

I protested that I was older and he knew it. But I smiled anyway.

"I may not look the same," I said, "but I feel the same, I think. I've missed you so much, too."

I took his arm and held it close as we walked out.

Every bite of my aged Delmonico steak with green peppercorn sauce was a delight. He'd chosen the restaurant, one of the new crop of chic, expensive, nouveau places in the city. Steak was the specialty, so I dove in. No ladylike salad for me! In my line, and being single anyway, I often eat alone, but now noticed how much more flavor every bite seemed to have. Or maybe it was my charming dining partner himself who enhanced the flavors of the food.

Ion asked me how I liked my steak. "I see you now eat beef blood rare. You *have* changed, after all." And he laughed a little.

"My palate and interests have changed, yes," I said. "But the essential things have stayed the same. I am the sum total of my memories, I guess."

Ion was now Minister of Education. The current president, a reformer, had appointed him. "I feel as if I can do good there on a large scale. More than I could do as a crusading journalist." He laughed at himself and his old identity of heroic reformer. "Now I'm one of the entrenched leadership I used to expose for their crimes."

He told me he had copies of two of my older books, one in English, one a French translation. "Why have you taken so long to have a Romanian translation?" he asked, teasing.

"Publishers," I said. "They want to know that your books will sell before they go all out. And besides, had I come sooner you wouldn't have been free to see me."

He looked straight at me. "Yes," he said. "And if you had,

and you were once in my sights, I might have been unable to restrain myself."

I felt like time had collapsed and we were back being young and full of fire. Time could be quite surreal. We were easy with each other. Conversation almost seemed to be restarting from moments ago rather than near decades. It was the same, the same. I swirled the wine in my glass and polished it off in one swallow. My stomach felt warm and my head a little tingly. I waved off the suggestion of dessert.

"I couldn't possibly," I said.

Ion had a driver, a surprise in itself. He ushered us into the car, and pulled out so smoothly I didn't feel the motion at all. Even though the driver was up front, I felt like we were completely alone. Somehow we managed not to undress each other in the damn car, but it took some effort.

When I felt his hand pulling me out of the back seat, I didn't even know or care where we were. The driver disappeared. We kissed in the elevator, a long kiss on a long ride. At the top, doors opened onto a private apartment. I'd notice the details tomorrow, but for now just noted that it looked expensive.

It took no time to undress each other. And then all of our old ways of touching were just the same, just right. I felt that transcendence that was like falling into a vortex, like the body collapsing in on itself like a star.

We lay in the dark, speaking quietly, though no one else was there.

"I've been reading your book, the new one about offal. It's a fascinating thing to read, a little unsettling, but a little forbidden, too, and therefore oddly stimulating. And your style is so unequivocal and erudite—no comic asides, no cuteness. Of course, I know you wouldn't do that sort of thing. But the subject matter in someone else's hands would probably be done tongue in cheek, I think you say in English."

I laughed. Ion hadn't changed. "I need you to write a review of my book," I said. "Some critics missed the point."

"But most didn't. I saw some very good notices." He paused. "And you eat this food, this offal?" I noted happily that he had resisted the pun. He loved English puns. He claimed it was the best language for punning and double entendres.

"Yes, I'm interested in it for several reasons. It comes from what used to be called 'peasant fare,' because the masses couldn't afford the top cuts. So the women who cooked the dishes made of sweetmeats and other now discarded parts created food with intense flavors. Some, I'm not that fond of, like brains. But I want to try everything. I want to understand what peoples in the past ate. And why people now still eat it."

"Why do you want this?"

I thought for a moment. "I want to regain some sense of food in the past so that I can understand food culture today." I thought about this, what I had just said, and decided it was too … scholastic-sounding. So I tried again: "Human experience is the sum total of the past. The past is who we are. If we can recover some fragments of it and understand them clearly, maybe we will understand how we got here and who we are now." I still wasn't satisfied with my comment, but felt I'd gotten closer.

"You're very ambitious. You used to talk about becoming famous."

I laughed quietly again. "I know I made an obnoxious statement on that subject when I was a young person. I'm happy now to publish my books and articles, and have a place in the world, doing what interests me. I make a living, and hope readers like what I do. I don't believe I could do anything but write."

"Not obnoxious. You have a special talent, and deserve the attention. I hope that someday it will come."

I thought about Ion's own brush with fame. His years as a committed journalist. At one time, people talked of Ion Vadim as a possible contender for the Prize. But it had never happened.

"You're famous," I said. "Everyone in Romania knows who you are."

"No, not anymore. It's really true—I'm just a bureaucrat now. People forget. And they should forget some things. I'm no longer that person."

I was surprised to hear him say this. I was certain he still did good, and said so.

And then Ion laughed. "But this is a gloomy subject! And why am I whispering, as if someone can hear us? Like in the old days, with the room bugged, and the Dictator's spies listening at the keyhole! Let's talk about something else. Tell me about your time here, what you're up to." His old self had returned.

I recited the program, first my talking tour of Transylvania, and then back to Bucharest for a talk in the National Gallery, and then on another trip to the northern and eastern side of the country. I mentioned the name Dick Elbow, and we laughed together. I then said that in Bucharest I would give a talk in the Cozma Cabinet.

"I'm counting on you being there," I murmured.

His laugh had died down. "The Cozma Cabinet," he said quietly, "in the National Gallery. I've read about it coming here. Why are you doing a talk there?"

I told him, though not all, saving up some for the talk itself. I would be talking about a newly discovered art piece Cozma had willed to the Romanian National Gallery. I told him about the images I'd seen of it. "It's called *Last Supper*. It's a sculpture of a last supper, but not Christ's. It depicts a meal, with male figures devouring entrails and other traditionally castaway foods, all of them wearing masks. Behind the masks are grotesque animal faces. I'm most interested in the food they are eating, and will talk about that."

Ion listened in the dark silence, not moving.

"I'll be there," he said. "I'll see you in the Cabinet."

I listened to the silence. "You don't seem very enthusiastic about my talk."

Ion said nothing for a moment, and then, "No, Vita, it's not that. Some feel that Cozma was a traitor. He ditched the country in its time of need. People say we needed all of our greatest artists and intellectuals. But I'm sure your talk will be engaging. I'll definitely be there."

As Ion dozed, I lay there, falling asleep and thinking about what he had said.

We slept tangled up in each other's limbs, on top of the mess of sheets, cooling from hot to warm. Breaths easing. And woke the same, tangled so it was hard to see where one body ended. Touched each other softly. Started up again.

I was supposed to be at the hotel soon for Radu to pick me up, but found it very difficult to say no to "just one more." When Ion finally let me get up and into the shower, I knew I was probably already late. So what difference would a few more minutes be?

When I emerged from the gorgeous modern bathroom— three times the size of my own, with a walk-in tiled shower you could play handball in and every luxury you could name—Ion handed me a café crème, the way I'd always liked it. Dark, strong coffee, rich cream, no sugar.

"Mmmm," I murmured. "I feel wonderful. I feel … feel, perfect."

He reached for the towel, but this time I insisted.

"I have to go. I *have* to. I made promises and I like to keep them. But tonight?"

"No," he said. "I'm sorry. I should have told you. I have to leave Bucharest today and will be gone for several days. But I will be at your talk in the Cozma Cabinet."

7

I walked into the hotel lobby, and there was Radu, sitting on a sofa looking at his cell phone. He looked up at me curiously, seeing my disheveled condition and my obvious evening outfit. He smiled and said hello.

I laughed, and said, "I may be getting old, but I'm not dead."

Radu looked a little embarrassed. "Yes … No. Of course."

He was there to see if I would like to do a little sightseeing, as we had talked about. I apologized to him for having to make the trip all the way out there, but said I was going to bed for a while, that I still needed to recover from the jet lag. He said he had been working at his university "faculty," only a block away, anyway, so it was no trouble.

I still wanted to join him and his friends on the town in the evening, though. Radu would return at an agreed-on hour, and take me out to meet some interesting friends and colleagues.

I went up to my room, feeling drained but happy. I kicked off my shoes, peeled off my dress, turned off the lights, and slid under the cool sheets.

It was late afternoon before I awoke. I knew this instinctively, without having to look at my watch on the bed stand.

My biorhythms were still out of kilter, or whatever the expression should be. I parted the blackout curtains and turned on the TV, trying to wake up entirely.

I came across a show with native folk music and dancing. While making myself a cup of coffee, I watched it. After the kooky musical performance ended, another equally puzzling music show came on, but it didn't seem like folk music. A dark man with earrings in dark suit, leering and grinning, sang to two young women in skin-tight clothes, the standing women slowly swaying their hips to the music. The music was repetitive and cloying, and sounded a bit like rap. I had never seen anything like it before.

Beginning to feel hungry, I showered, and, dressed rather casually, in dark jeans, short boots and a brown sweater, eventually made my way downstairs to the café. I sat down and had a mineral water and club sandwich, waiting for Radu.

He showed up on time, greeting me in his warm manner. He was parked out front, so we walked through the front doors, past the doorman. The man watched as Radu, speaking quietly to them, gave some change to the Gypsy panhandlers.

Radu drove to Lipscani, the charming old commercial and artisan guild district built during the Middle Ages, and now a fashionable quarter and tourist destination.

"Lipscani didn't look like this when I was last here. It was almost completely devastated."

"The communists planned on demolishing it and putting up some more of their 'modern' architecture," Radu said, "but lucky for us never got around to it."

We met up with Radu's friends at a bar smartened up in the style of a grand Left Bank café that reminded me of one of my favorite Paris haunts, so I felt curiously both here and there.

"We young Romanians have a lot of nostalgia for the period

between the wars, when Bucharest was still the 'Paris of the East.'"

The group of people, all seated at a table, smiled up at me as Radu introduced them. He presented a roommate, Mihai, a nice-looking young man who was working on his doctoral degree at the university. In "philology," I understood Radu to say.

"Is that like the study of literature?" I asked the grad student.

"Yes," Mihai said. "It's the study of language in texts."

I had no idea what that meant, but let the introductions go on.

Next was Magda, his other roommate, a smart-looking young woman, wearing chic glasses, with a raven's wing of black hair across her forehead. She was a new assistant professor of Art History at the university.

"I've been reading your book," she said. *The Story of Offal.* It's a brilliant cultural study of food. I'm already thinking of ways to include it in my classes."

I was both startled and pleased to hear this.

"That's very pleasant to hear, but I find it a little strange to think of my book being used in a college class *in Romania*!" And I laughed.

They gazed at me. And Magda said, "You have a great laugh!"

I smiled.

Finally, Radu introduced an attractive woman, somewhat older than himself and the rest, with short blond hair. "This is Ana. Ana is a curator at the National Gallery, and she's the one who arranged the Cozma Cabinet. Ana is also my girlfriend."

Delighted, I sat down next to Ana, saying, "Oh, how wonderful! I am captivated by *Last Supper*. It's held a special fascination for me since I first saw photographs of it several years ago. And now I'm going to be doing a talk in the Cozma Cabinet. I'm very excited about it."

"Only the most famous writers read and talk at the National Gallery," Ana said.

"I'm not famous," I said, and laughed.

Ana told me that along with the almost entirely unseen art pieces, Cozma had passed on many boxes of sketches, plans, diagrams, personal papers, and extensive documentation about the art itself. "Madga, Mihai, Radu, and I have been given the mind-blowing job of going through this mountain of material and trying to make sense of it all."

Ana spoke excitedly about the work the four were doing.

"This is the most important project any of us has ever worked on. It's boxes and boxes. It's taken us months already just to sort and catalog about half of them. Every time we open a box we hold our breaths, mad to uncover the secrets within."

Ana rubbed her hands together and attempted a fiendish laugh, which was so incongruous on her that it made everyone else laugh.

"This is some of the work on the patrimony that Radu told me about," I said, and the others nodded.

Radu was sitting on the other side of Ana, and I noted that their arms brushed and they touched each other casually, a sign of a couple in a comfortable relationship. Even if Radu hadn't introduced her as his girlfriend, it would have been obvious.

I ordered a beer and talked about my past experiences in Romania while the others smoked and ordered the next round. I'd traveled around Transylvania, and I'd gone to the Black Sea and Danube Delta, on the eastern side of the country.

"Oh, I love it there!" Magda said.

I repeated what I'd told Radu, about everything being so different. There were no chic shops and cafés, no shiny new western European cars and western-style supermarkets. But, somehow, it seemed the same to me, underneath.

"We say that the mentality hasn't changed," Madga said. "Most of the people running the government are the same ones who ran it during the communist period. This time they're lining their pockets even more than they did under the old system. And Romanians think in the same way they did before. In some ways nothing has changed, except that now we are open to the outside, and we have a 'free' economy."

Ana said, "We are afraid that our patrimony is under threat."

I wanted to hear more about this idea of the patrimony, and asked the group to clarify what it meant.

"It's everything that makes up our identity as a society and nation," Ana said. "It's the opera, symphony, all kinds of Romanian classical and modern music. It's high painting, sculpture—like Cozma's—as well as the folk arts."

I recalled the show I'd watched on TV earlier, the folk music and dancing, and described it.

Everyone nodded. These were commercial versions of what Ana was talking about, the music their parents had liked.

"Now that I think of it, I saw two different music shows. The first was folk music, with women wearing traditional costume, and in the second the singers looked like Gypsies to me. And the music sounded a little like rap." I smiled, unsure if that made sense.

"Yes, there's a popular, kind of Gypsy rap music now," Madga said. "It's very sexist. And it's grossly commercial, and not really anything like traditional Romani music."

Ana said, "I don't think that that music is indicative of Romani people. It's just the same old fantasies about Gypsies and sex."

I observed an intriguing occurrence. Magda and Mihai

looked at Radu, yet said nothing. And Radu looked at his glass of beer. I didn't know what was going on between them all.

I asked whether Romani people were abusing their own culture in this case, but, again, no one answered. I couldn't understand their reticence. In the past, Romanians were always ready to express their opinions about the Gypsies.

"I see what you mean by the attitude being essentially the same," I said, "but I think your generation is quite different than the past. In the past, Romanians didn't talk about Gypsies in a very kind light."

"We're not typical of our generation, either," Magda said. "We're more progressive. Radu, Ana, Mihai, and I are the Four Musketeers."

Radu said it was time to move on to our next destination. The five of us managed to pile into Radu's car, but the trip was short, and young Romanians are invariably skinny. We went to a cavernous room behind the National Gallery, where music performances took place and non-commercial films were shown to young audiences. I had another beer, and listened to a famed Romanian jazz saxophonist playing standards with his combo. Radu's group smoked and talked while the music played.

When Radu saw me watching him smoking, he said, "I'm quitting next week!" and laughed.

"No need for explanations," I said. "I smoked for many years and enjoyed the heck out of it. I thought of bumming one from you, in fact."

He held out the pack, and I hesitated, and then took one. What the heck.

Soon another young man with a shaved head joined the group, an American named Larry Something-or-other, who was attached to a nonprofit. With the music playing, I didn't catch his last name, and it was too late to ask once we'd gotten talking. Radu said to the shaved-head Larry that he should meet me, a visiting dignitary and writer.

Larry sat down next to me and asked what I was doing in Romania. I told him a little of the story, with some highlights about my book. I had to speak loudly to be heard over the bebop.

The guy took a swig from his beer bottle and said, "Id'n that kind of ridiculous? I mean, the Romanians don't really have a cuisine. They just have bland, fattening food, and they add greasy French fries to it. I just eat at the McDonald's all the time. Do you think Romanians are going to care much about your book?" He gave me a reptilian smile, which disconcertingly complemented his hairless pate.

"I don't know. Romanians cook with all parts of an animal. Or they used to." I didn't really want to talk to this guy.

He had that kind of know-it-all American male voice: "Well, what are your sources? What kind of stuff are you relying on for that?" He clearly assumed that my books were baloney.

I was going to tell him more, but decided there was no point in it. I excused myself and went to the women's room, and when I returned sat down at the part of the table where Radu and Ana were.

"What do you think of Larry?" Ana was smiling meaningfully. "He sat down with us here one night when we were with a British friend and heard us speaking English, and he has kind of attached himself to us. I think he likes Magda."

"I think what we have here is a character from a Hitchcock classic. The man who knew too much."

Radu and Ana laughed. And so did I.

Cleanhead at the other end of the table looked at me, the know-it-all expression on his face changing to a look of incomprehension.

We were all kind of drunk.

"To the patrimony!" Ana called out, raising her glass.

"The patrimony!" Radu, Magda, and Mihai chimed in.

I hadn't raised my glass. "I don't know about that word."

Ana said, "What word?"

"*Patrimony*," I said, looking at the young people. "It sounds like you're working to preserve the *patriarchy*. Can't you come up with a better word?"

Everyone looked at me in astonishment. And then burst out laughing.

And Ana yelled, "Okay, then, to the *matrimony*!"

Beer rushed out of my nose, as I nearly choked on it, to everyone's delight. Regaining myself and raising my glass, I called out, "To the Four Musketeers!"

It was obviously the beginning of an evening of drunken hilarity. For me, their jet-lagged senior, it was the end. I told Radu I would take a taxi back to the hotel. He protested in a halfhearted way, but this time, looking over at the beautiful Ana, let me prevail.

8

The next day Radu drove me to the TV station, a large, squat building near the Consulate, with massive aerial towers on the roof.

Inside, I was introduced to the director, a bespectacled, sleepy-looking young man who greeted me in English. The director said there was really only one rule. I should not speak unless asked a question.

I then met the show's host. He said he was a cultural critic, and asked me about New York, his favorite city in the world. I said I came from Los Angeles, but liked New York very much. After that, he didn't seem to be very interested in me.

And then I was introduced to my translator, a young woman with a degree from the university. The woman was pretty, and spoke with a British accent.

I sat in a comfortable chair under glaring lights. I was keyed up, but ready.

The host asked me why I wrote cookbooks.

"I don't write cookbooks. I have several friends who have written wonderful cookbooks, but that isn't something I do myself."

The man didn't seem to hear my response. He talked about the idea of cookbooks, how in Romania they weren't necessary because recipes were handed down through generations.

When he was done, I recounted my reasoning in writing *Snouts, Tails, Entrails,* answering the question I'd anticipated. "I became interested in the subject many years ago. In fact, my past experience in Romania partly contributed to my interest."

The host was unaware that I had lived in Romania during the pre-transition period, and, looking remote, he asked me to elaborate. I talked about the way in which in the past Romanians, like most Europeans, had used every part of an animal. It was a food culture that naturally exploited offal. "In effect, this is its cultural heritage, part of the Romanian *patrimony.*" Suddenly the word seemed appropriate. I gave some concrete examples to illustrate my point.

While I was doing this, the host was smiling in a plainly patronizing manner. He replied that Romanians have always looked to the French for their food culture, just as they looked to the French for architecture and painting, philosophy and literature, education and fashion. "Our entire *patrimony* is directly attributable to French influence," he said. He talked

41

about the Romanian love of fine cooking and food preparation. The French sauces and *saucisson*. He seemed on the verge of challenging me, relying on the Romanian affection for everything French to suggest that my argument was invalid.

Loving a meaty discussion, I dove in, saying that this was in reality a myth about Romanians. The middle and upper classes looked to the French for their cultural models, but the majority of Romanians, who were either farmers or had direct rural connections, didn't. I gave a few key examples of the Romanian usage of snouts, tails, innards, feet, vitals, and everything else. I talked about *drob*, the sort of Romanian haggis, an essential dish made at Easter, and made of entrails.

"In any case, the French were a profoundly offal-based culture," I said. I gave a few key examples of French offal-use practice.

"In fact," I continued, "*saucisson sec* is an excellent example of French offal culture. The French style sausage made with pork fat-back and cased in pig intestine has an ancient genealogy. There are Roman and Gaulish recipes. In French literature, the first mention of *saucisson sec* is in the 16th century, in fact. Rabelais mentions it in *Tiers livres*." This was all in my book, I told him.

As for Romanians, I went on, research showed that regardless of class until recently all ate all kinds of foods that would now be routinely thrown away. I could hear the translator chattering, keeping up with my commentary.

Delighted to talk on this subject, I laughed.

The studio was completely silent. The host looked taken aback. The interpreter had stopped chattering, and was gawking at me.

I looked around. The cameraman peered out from behind his camera. The lighting person's mouth was a little open. The guy in the sound booth craned his neck to get a good look at me. The bespectacled director stood by, now looking awake.

I thought my comments may have offended somehow. A little anxious, I laughed again.

The host seemed flustered. He began in Romanian, then, realizing what he'd been doing, changed back to English. His neck reddened increasingly as he talked. The translator interpreted what he was saying to the Romanian audience. Basically, it amounted to a brief lecture on Romanian culture, the man starting with the ancient Dacians, the forerunners of the modern Romanians, and then moving through the Medieval period, and then on to the modern era and the arrival of Romanian national identity, with a fleeting nod to the communist time, and finally a comment on the present, which he referred to as the "post-transition" period. As if he had some special knowledge that everyone else in the country didn't share.

Whatever point he intended to make about Romanian food had not been made, though he seemed to think it had. He looked at me, his eyes narrowed.

Meanwhile, I had remembered that I was not supposed to speak unless asked a question. I grinned at the man.

But he didn't ask a question, and the interview ended. The camera drew back. The host was perspiring a little under the bright lights.

As Radu drove me back to my hotel, he said, "You did something Romanians all across the country have wanted to see for many years! You put that offal-eating gasbag in his place! Oh, my God, what a thing to see!" He was laughing, honking the car horn as he drove down the busy city thoroughfare.

I was a bit alarmed and concerned. "That wasn't my intention. I like a good discussion, and assumed he did, too. He evidently had a lot invested in the topic. I must have come off as very arrogant."

"No, no!" Radu said. "You were charming. I was watching through the TV monitor. You have that rare quality of someone who really—I can't quite think of the word—*commands* video. Your personality really comes through beautifully. It's because you're so animated, I guess, and spontaneous. We have never seen that kind of thing on this cultural program. It's all just talking heads. *Spontaneity!* And life! And your wonderful laugh. You were delightful!"

The next day I would begin the first leg of my tour, of the Transylvanian cities. Not convinced by Radu's attempt to reassure me, I hoped no one who came to the talks would have seen the interview.

PART II

1

A chilly morning, and I had to rise early to catch the train to Braşov, a Transylvanian city surrounded by the southern Carpathian mountains, with its massive, gloomy Gothic cathedral and a popular ski resort, where I would be speaking. Radu was waiting in the hotel café at the agreed-on 6:30, his hands wrapped around a hot cup of coffee.

He laughed when he saw me. I looked at him and then laughed, too. I no doubt looked like I could fall back into bed. He'd ordered me a coffee, as well, which went down in one gulp.

On this frosty, early morning no Romani women and children loitered at the front doors of the hotel. But several taxis idled in a queue, awaiting fares. Radu asked the sizeable doorman to bring a taxi forward. While the man was motioning a driver to pull forward, Radu whispered to me, "I wonder why they dress like one of the Tzar's cavalry officers."

It made me snicker.

We were on our way to the station. I watched several dogs crossing the streets, trotting alongside passersby.

Radu had secured our tickets the night before, so we bypassed the sluggish lines at the ticket counters and entered the massive old fortress-like station at one of the checkpoints. Police rummaged though others' bags, but when the guard dressed in camo saw me, he motioned with his black automatic weapon for us to come through. The cops glanced at our tickets, my passport, and Radu's national identity card, and we were inside.

Radu said, "You have the magical blue passport."

Inside the station, we had time for another coffee. Radu said, "We should go the McDonald's. It's very American," and laughed. We sat at a McDonald's, having another coffee and a pastry. We could munch on our pastry al fresco, as the place had tables outside under the roof of the enormous, open-air station. We sat watching the bustle of the station, chatting pleasantly. I enjoy this kind of thing immensely.

Radu had gotten up considerably earlier than I had because he had to take the metro to the hotel. While I was simply tired, he was sleep-deprived. I wished I had insisted he take a taxi instead, I said, but he, smiling and waving a hand, would hear none of it. I knew he wouldn't have taken money from me for a taxi.

I recalled how it could get a little complicated with Romanians and money if you tried to pay for something. I sensed that it would be very easy to offend them, even and probably especially if they didn't have much money.

"The metro system is quite good here in Bucharest," Radu said brightly, as if reading my mind. "We have to admit it's the one of the few things the mad communist regime did well."

I liked the Britishism: *mad.* "I remember it," I said. "It's more dependable than the London tube or Paris metro. And it's certainly more reliable than the New York subway!" I threw back my head and laughed.

Some passengers waiting at a neighboring table looked over at me.

We talked about rapid transit in Los Angeles, with me having to admit that it was highly inadequate, as people wanted to be in their own cars.

Radu then looked a bit abstracted when an announcement came over the PA system. Embarrassed a little that I had learned almost no Romanian, I didn't speak. When the announcement ceased, Radu said we must catch our train.

The train was nicer than those I'd taken in the past, though passengers still smoked, the windows shut. The heat was on, and, as it was a nippy morning, the warmth felt good.

Radu smiled in apology for his lassitude and snoozed. Despite my fatigued state, I couldn't sleep, so watched the landscape go by, laptop on my knees.

Outside of Bucharest, the environment changed from urban wasteland to villages and farmlands.

Eventually the train rose in elevation, and the scenes became comparatively more pleasant. Or maybe this was because the sun came out finally and shone on the pastures and rocky hills, giving a crystalline quality to everything. I regained the spirits of the early morning, and looked forward to my talk.

Brașov was as I remembered it, with the colossal Black Church glowering over one end of the lovely old city's vast square. The cathedral's gloomy countenance didn't seem to be improved by the bright sunshine.

We met our hosts at a café on the square. Mr. Blaga, the resort manager, and Mrs. Popescu, his assistant, shook my hand warmly. With the outdoor heaters blowing, we were able to sit at a small table outside. Mr. Blaga said, "We are so happy to meet you finally. We are so very glad you here." He laughed, and said, "Please excuse my English. It is very rude."

Mrs. Popescu said, "Our generation force to study Russian for many years, but nobody want to do now. Can't remember no more Russian!" she said laughing, gesturing to indicate that nothing could be done about this. "Now we try to learn English, like the young people," indicating Radu.

"You're doing admirably!" I said. "I can't speak Romanian, and I'm in your country. Anyway, if we run into a hitch, Radu here can act as translator." I laughed.

They looked at Radu, and he said something in Romanian. No doubt what I had just said.

After another and welcome café crème, we got into Mr.

Blaga's gleaming German car and headed up the mountain to have lunch, after which would come my talk at the resort. I was famished! All I'd had was the pastry at the train station McDonald's. "I have to admit," I said. "I can eat like a horse. And once or twice I've eaten horse!"

Mr. Blaga listened to Radu's translation of my comment, nodded, and said, "Romanians not eat horse."

I was taken to a revered old, rustic-style Romanian restaurant, with rough wooden tables and benches. An assortment of animals' heads hung on the walls, overlooking the scene, their eyes vacant. The menu listed all manner of game, including wild boar, which I ordered. I'd had it before and was curious how it would be served in the Romanian style.

"I hope it's not *boaring*!" Radu said.

"Oh, my God," I said, "that's the worst pun I've ever heard."

He beamed.

Mr. Blaga and Mrs. Popescu didn't get it, and Radu tried to explain.

The food was described as "traditional Dacian," the Dacians being the ancient ancestors of the Romanians. Radu said to me, "The Dacians were the people Ovid loathed for their uncouth ways."

I was interested in the idea that contemporary Romanians would want to reproduce how their ancient ancestors prepared food.

Radu asked how contemporary Romanians could know what the Dacians ate. He was grinning, a little puckishly.

Mr. Blaga said, "It is known from history. The Dacians were our ancestors, and we eating the same food they did eat." Though smiling, he seemed a little miffed by the question.

Otherwise, the conversation was lively, and I enjoyed myself, relating some of my former experiences in Romania. My hosts were surprised that I'd been to their country during the time of the old regime. Radu watched me intently as I recounted my narratives, laughing heartily at my experiences in the then surreal socialist country. I then talked about how different nearly everything was now, how prosperous much of it looked. Radu said something in Romanian here and there, clarifying a point I'd made.

"Yes," Mr. Blaga said. "Things very different now. The resort doing very well. Very popular with skiers from all places, not only Romania. Germany, England, France, Italy …" He seemed to be wearing down, tiring of speaking English.

"How was the boar?" Radu asked.

"It was fantastic!" I said. I had eaten all of my wild boar stew, which I suppose would have been several portions for an ordinary person. It had come with a mound of *mămăliga* in the center. The stew had been cooked in red wine, with a nice herby-spicy flavor and a bit of a chili kick. This was something I hadn't experienced in Romania before—I remembered most Romanians I'd known not liking spicy food. Though the meat was not beef, the preparation reminded me of a *boeuf bourguignon*. I had to stop myself from licking the bowl.

I asked my hosts to find out if I could talk to the chef. When he came out, large and pink-faced and looking curious, I said, "That was fantastic! I've had wild boar before, more than once, but this was so unique and delicious! I could die right now and be content with my last meal."

I asked if we could offer him a glass, considering it was the slow time between lunch and dinner.

He sat down, and took the glass of white wine with a grin. I was pleased to see that when Radu explained who I was, the chef got very excited.

"Tell her I am reading her book!" he said. "I wish I had it

with me now! I would want her to sign it for me."

"Here," I said, pulling a copy from my bag. "I always carry a few copies to give to special friends."

I inscribed the book, "To a divine artist of cuisine, who wields spices and knives like paints and brushes to create a masterpiece for the palate."

As he listened to the translation, the chef's cheeks grew pinker, his grin grew broader, and he rose and bowed to me, took my hand and kissed it.

I laughed delightedly.

The resort was impressive—and a bit intimidating. A massive complex several floors high and easily an L.A. city block long. At this elevation, snow clung to the roof. I hugged myself as I was ushered into the building and then into a vast conference room, large enough for hundreds.

About thirty people sat at tables, watching me walk in. Some were dressed in food prep white, no doubt staff from the resort's restaurant.

Radu stood by, ready to translate. I relaxed when I saw the small group.

"Thank you for the marvelous introduction," I said, nodding to my hosts and smiling broadly at the crowd, which included among the white coats a mixed bag of older men in sport coats, white-haired women wearing high heels, and students in blue jeans and boots. Not a large crowd but not bad for a book talk in a ski village during the off-season.

"I am grateful for the kind way my homecoming has been received in Romania. For, yes, this is a homecoming. I've not been back in Romania for many years, and have been looking forward to this day for a long time. So many things have changed, but there is still *mici*, still *țuică*, still Dacias, still warm-hearted people and intelligent dogs."

After the light laughter died down, I continued.

"Let me introduce my translator, Radu Luca, a graduate student at the University of Bucharest. He is a very bright young man, a cultural historian. Remember him. Trust me, you will all know his name some day."

This I spoke in Romanian, having written it out and practiced saying it with Ion till my pronunciation no longer drew a headshake or a sigh.

Radu, beaming and reddening simultaneously, bowed to me.

I cleared my throat, gathered myself, and launched into the talk, some from notes, some from my head, some read from my book.

"Everything old is new again. I imagine there is a similar expression in Romanian, and that sentiment is especially true in this country. The heart of my recent book, so to speak, is the history and recent popularization of eating offal—all of those normally discarded parts of an animal, internal organs and entrails, the parts that don't make up a steak or a chop. I just ate lunch at your renowned local restaurant where Dacian food is served. As were virtually all ancient cultures, the early Romanians were eaters of internal organs, and their rituals, for harvest and other ceremonies, were offal dishes.

"But while offal is my subject, I see this and other recent trends as related: related to the 'farm to table' movement, to the 'real food' movement, to natural and organic and local and all backwards-looking trends, and to environmental concerns about our food choices and processes.

"Ever since people began migrating from rural to urban areas, there's been nostalgia for that supposed idyllic past, when people enjoyed 'simple' pleasures, ones that were hardly simple to enjoy, considering all of the steps it took just to get a loaf of bread, for example! Growing the grain, harvesting, milling, grinding finely enough to make flour, leavening, proofing, shaping, baking. Good lord, but I think I would have just given up and stuck to eating whatever I could pluck wild from shrubs and trees! Part of the nostalgia for old ways was and is a reaction to speed and convenience, two ideas that were dominant when I was a kid.

"We can all agree, I think, that we modern people are distant now from the circle of life of our food, the seasons. The conditions that are right to grow a pumpkin are different from those that are good for asparagus. This is a simple fact, but we do not know it instinctively anymore because foods come to us from the world, regardless of the season we are in. Transportation makes it possible to eat strawberries in the winter in a temperate climate like that of, say, Minnesota, USA, which gets as cold as Braşov in the dead of winter, even colder.

I paused a moment while the crowd murmured and stirred, as if surprised that there were such cold and inhospitable environs in the United States.

"I'm thankful for this access. I couldn't make my beloved Greek *avogolemono* soup without lemons, and a hot, rich soup is just better in the winter than the summer."

I'm told that when I get going my voice becomes modulated like a preacher's. I fall into a state where there is nothing but my voice and the words. Friends tell me that audiences become mesmerized, and if that's right, I thought it was true with this one no less, despite the simultaneous translation that slowed it down a little.

"Far from believing this is a bad thing, I'm overjoyed to buy *jamon ibérico* from Spain and Camembert from France. I can't imagine how their lack would impoverish my life. I love that I live in the age of food, and all of the foods I have mentioned are certainly real.

"Here is one counterexample, though: oleomargarine, which my grandmother Edna, a funny, big-hearted woman with a big, infectious laugh, called 'oleo' for short. Even the name is unappealingly processed-sounding, and no wonder. It was created in a lab, way back in the 19th century by a Frenchman—the irony!

"I'm sure many of you here have made butter. It couldn't be simpler, right? Pour heavy cream into a jar, shake till the curds separate from the whey, drain—save the whey, the buttermilk, for soups and so on—add salt if you want. There. Done. Now oleomargarine is made in a lab in a process that extracts oils from plant materials—cottonseed, canola seed, et cetera—then partially hydrogenates it to make it solid.

"Here is a list of ingredients in one common brand of margarine found in every American grocery store: liquid and partially hydrogenated soybean oil, soy lecithin, potassium sorbate, mono and diglycerides …"

Radu threw up his hands and looked at me with an expression that said, *I have no idea how to translate that into Romanian!*

I stopped speaking, looked at his crestfallen face, and said, "Oh! You don't know the Romanian words for these things! I see! Be proud of that!"

Then I turned to the audience.

"I'm afraid I sprang this list on my very talented translator"—Radu bowed to the audience—"just before coming on, this crazy list of very unfood words.

"Maybe these, not being ingredients in real food, need no translation. Of them, how many are recognizable as foods? Maybe three? Water, buttermilk, oil. Contents of butter: cream, with or without salt. We all know what real food is. It is food made from real ingredients that we recognize as food.

"The irony of speaking here is that the previous time I was in your country, I was fed homegrown vegetables, fruits, *ahhh*, the divine tomatoes! Wine came from grapes grown at the family's country house.

"I know this is still true for many of you, but I imagine even you fear the end of these traditions. You still grow and press and eat and drink what is grown on land your family owns. And most of you still do a large part of your food shopping at the fantastic open markets. But the distance between consumer and food source is growing even here. In recent years, agro-tourism inns have sprung up here and in other countries to capitalize on our modern distance from the source, to take us back to our origins as growers and eaters.

"In addition to the old food ways, I'm sure many of you have all-too-strong memories of hunger during the food shortages you had to live through. Food. It's the center of our lives. It feeds and nurtures us, it causes pain and wars. It can degrade or be created in harmony with nature. It can exploit or help to sustain the humans who work to produce it."

I went on a bit longer, explaining about my interest in offal, about how I'd often been offered—and twice ate—sautéed brain during my previous time in Romania, how the country life made it impractical to throw away any animal parts that couldn't be somehow used. And how the latest, trendiest restaurants in the States and in the UK now offered up dishes of entrails and marrow at high prices.

It had been a long day, and I longed for a taste of the waiting wine and cheese, but took Q&A with aplomb.

The first query came from a woman in a white food preparer's uniform. She wanted to know how tall I was. Everyone laughed.

"This is one of the questions I get asked the most," I said. "I am 6'3". In centimeters, that's 190.5. I come from a tall family, and I did play a little basketball in high school. Height has its advantages! I tend to get served first at bars. On the other hand, the cute, trendy platform shoes, alas, I just can't wear. I'm afraid I'd look like Frankenstein's monster."

The audience laughed.

The second questioner, an older man, posed a quite different query.

"You say many of us remember the food shortages of the previous era," he said. "We do. Someone I know was imprisoned for growing and eating carrots. Carrots! Yes, food is much more than something to eat. It is politics. It is life and death. What I want to ask, Miss Unwin, is this. Have you ever been hungry? I mean hungry for a long stretch of time, not the casual way people say it today. I mean hungry so that you can't sleep for the emptiness in your stomach, and you worry about your children. Have you ever been hungry like that?"

I didn't flinch. But my mind traveled back to what was a hungry time for me. When sometimes all I had was water and a shaker of salt.

"Yes, I was young and I lived in one of the most fantastic food cities in the world. You see, I went to Paris to study art. I worked for a year waiting tables in my hometown to save the money to move there. I had romantic notions of myself in a garret, surrounded by books of art and sketchbooks full of my own renderings, as if I could afford books and sketchbooks. I could barely afford the rent for my barren little room, with its chest of drawers, chair, sunken bed, and sink, and the bathroom down two flights of stairs.

"I'd expected to get work soon after I arrived. My savings were not great, and I only intended to use them to get to Paris and for initial expenses. But it took months for me to find any real work, which ended up being copyediting text meant for an expatriate English-speaking readership. My employer was a bit 'sketchy,' as everyone says today, and there were rumors about him having some sort of violent past.

"But, as usual, I digress. Before I landed that job, I would gaze into the store and restaurant windows brimming with pastries and chocolates and meats, gape at the market tables overflowing with gorgeous fruit and vegetables. I envisioned myself like a waif—a very tall waif!—in a Charlie Chaplin film, tattered and wasting.

"Paris, being hungry in Paris, I suppose, is what turned my thoughts and focus away from the study and creation of art as a profession and toward food. I thought then that I would like to know about food, about the histories of individual foods, about the way tastes develop differently in different cultures, about the way simple ingredients can come together into a creation of exquisite, layered, complex, and thrilling flavors.

"What I am saying is that Paris was a revelation for me. The products themselves, the careful preparation, the artistry of presentation. It was a very hard place in which to be broke and hungry. I really did live on bread and cheap *cave* wine for weeks at a time. But my eyes and ears and nose took it all in.

"I will never forget my first real meal after receiving my pay—a demi-baguette that crackled perfectly when I squeezed it, a little crock of butter, a small roast chicken, juicy and herby and aromatic, a crunchy, lemony carrot salad, a petite strawberry tart, and a bottle of Burgundy. I carefully placed each piece, each wrapped like a present, in my tote basket, found a bench with a pleasant view of fountains, and unwrapped each and savored every bite. Gee, it still makes my mouth water. It was simple fare but at the same time far from simple. All done with care, to entice each of the senses.

"Well! No one will ever accuse me of brevity! And now all that talk of food has made me truly hungry, and thirsty! Shall we retreat to the reception room for some food and wine? I'll be happy to chat more with all of you, sign books, and so on. I do thank you for coming and for being such a wonderful audience!"

Mr. Blaga came to the front, made the usual thanks, and officially broke up the talk.

Finally, my long fingers curled around a glass of sublime red liquid—sublime to the thirsty, and also very tasty—I drank and felt myself unwinding, bit by bit. Beside me rested a nice plate of cheeses, bread, and pickled vegetables. I was told everything was local, and the pickles had been made by Mrs. Popescu.

"These are delightful!" I said, taking another crunchy bite of cauliflower. "Tangy and salty and just perfect to go with cheese. Will you share your recipe?"

Mrs. Popescu said, "Yes, of course, it is nothing, everyone makes pickles. It is just one way of many," and set off to find paper and pen on which to write it down. In spite of her claimed modesty, Mrs. Popescu couldn't entirely hide her pleasure.

The man who'd asked the question about hunger appeared before me, a well-used copy of one of my earlier books in hand, holding it out.

"Please, Miss Unwin. For my son, Ovidiu. He is a great fan, but works too hard and could not be here to witness your speech."

"Certainly, Mr. …"

"Eminescu," he said, with an old-worldish movement that made me think of a gentleman doffing his hat. "I am a farmer, you see. Or I was. I don't have much land left to farm. So now I work at a bookstore in town. I read, I remember, I try to make my son smile."

His own smile was conveyed across thin lips, but not so far as his eyes. There was an aura about him, an old sadness that refused to be erased. I'd seen the likes of it before, on Ion, on his face, in his eyes: the weight of an ugly history forever carried, imprinted on the body, like a scar. Time heals all wounds.

Bullshit, I said to myself.

"I thought your question shot right for the heart of things," I said. "This is what I remember of the nature of Romanian people—a seriousness, a curiosity, and a willingness to be critical. I miss that seriousness sometimes when I go on book tours in the States. There I often get more ingratiating questions that really don't say anything, or, I guess, ask anything. 'How do you come up with your ideas?' or 'Who is your favorite food writer?'

"Actually, to the last question, I have a ready answer: MFK Fisher, of course! Of food writers she is my first and last love. Back to the subject. People I encounter on tours rarely challenge the content of what I've written, or, especially, my right to write my subject."

Mr. Eminescu nodded.

"I once had a large farm," he said. "We grew and raised our food and sold it to restaurants. That was long ago. It was taken. My son now is in the business of food. He is chef at one of the top restaurants in Sinaia. You must go while you are in Romania. I'm sure my son would treat you especially well. I will tell him so! And he would love to meet you in person."

I hadn't thought about doing any additional traveling. The prospect made me nearly giddy with exhaustion. The great traveler who hated travel. Sometimes, I just wanted to stand still for a while.

I always forget—a good thing, considering—what international travel is really like. Waiting. Riding endlessly in cars, on crowded planes, trains, and buses, on boats. Sleeping in strange beds. Eating strange foods. Not having time to think, much less to run or to stretch. Being pushed and pulled.

But who knew. I took down the specific information and told Mr. Eminescu that I would do my best to get there.

I looked at the paper with the name Ovidiu Eminescu on it. Ovidiu. Like the poet. I loved that name. And the name of the wine I'd drunk with Ion. Lacrima de Ovidius, "The Tears of Ovid." Who else would name a wine that? And in Latin? It was charming, this pride of erudition. I was glad to see that Romania was still not among the countries where "dumbing down" was the model. I felt a little tired after my talk, but energized by the experience.

Clearly an important man, Mr. Blaga excused himself, saying he had work to attend to. In her Dacia, much newer than Radu's, Mrs. Popescu drove Radu and me back down the mountain to our hotel.

I learned that Mrs. Popescu's first name was Ștefania, and we had a nice chat on the way. Ștefania wanted to come to the United States, and asked a number of questions about New York. I said that I lived on the other side of the country, but would do my best to answer the questions. Ștefania was intent on knowing something about New York food markets and eateries, subjects I was able to talk about.

I knew that many Romanians regarded a visit to New York essential, like going to London or Paris. Los Angeles was a place that made movies.

"But the New York subway is undependable!" Radu said, interrupting from the backseat.

I laughed, too, and, strangely, Ştefania nearly drove off the mountain road and into a canyon.

2

The next day Radu and I rose early in our separate rooms at the hotel, a newly renovated place near the train station, and met for breakfast in the dining room. As I can really pack it in, and knowing that the ride to Cluj would be a long one, I had a large meal of eggs, tomatoes, bread, and sausage along with several cups of coffee.

The train was a new, special express that flew across the lush Transylvanian countryside. Luckily, it had a car with a small food concession, so for lunch we bought sandwiches and more coffee. As the cars rocked on the tracks, we tottered back through the train to first class, and lunched in our seats.

We sat in a pleasant sitting compartment with a multigenerational Romanian family. A grandfather, his daughter and her husband, and their little girl. The grandfather, dressed in suit and tie, wanted to tell me—clearly, a tourist—about the hops that grew in the fields we passed. He said they were made into a local brew that was very good. He was drinking some now. He showed me several bottles in a sack by his feet, and offered me one.

I sipped it while Radu translated the grandfather's lecture, occasionally smiling meaningfully at me. Radu evidently thought the old man was a little tiresome, but I was interested in hearing the lecture, attempting to comprehend as much as I could. I like hearing about the making of regional beverages and foods.

As he discoursed, the man lit a cigarette, a malodorous French Gauloise. The man's adult daughter, seeing me looking at his smoke and trying not to inhale, beseeched him to put the cigarette out, but he ignored her. The woman smiled repentantly at me and shrugged. Judging from the cut of his fine wool suit, he was a prosperous old patriarch and used to doing whatever he wanted to.

The woman's husband read a magazine and looked up once in a while, telling his little girl to stop being noisy. He once looked at Radu and me and nodded, but did not engage with us.

Soon the train traversed high mountainous areas, moving briskly along stunning, deeply forested gorges and glistening blue rivers, no doubt, I thought, teeming with trout.

Since the grandfather liked to hold forth about the region, I tried to ask the man about the regional fishing. "I am an avid fly angler," I told the old man through Radu, "and have fished in trout streams throughout the American West. I practice catch-and-release, but occasionally I let myself take a trout or two from a river. Nothing can compare with a trout taken fresh from a fast-moving stream, cleaned immediately, and then pan-fried in butter and salt on a campfire."

But he said he knew nothing about fishing and in fact didn't care for it. He lit another smelly smoke, and looked out the window at the mountain passes.

And then suddenly he said something, and Radu translated: "This is the real Transylvania!" A Transylvanian, he was proud.

Transylvania. In American pop culture it means Count Dracula. Sinister castles on ragged peaks, corpses quiescent in coffins, creepy guys in capes sucking the blood of attractive young women and then turning into bats and flapping eloquently into the night sky.

Vampires are part of the American popular culture. But Romanians, I know, are at best puzzled and sometimes exasperated when asked about them. They don't understand the

American fondness for vampires, and resent the fact that, if an American knows anything at all about Romania, it has to be Count Dracula. The story of the real man is bizarre enough, without the mythic narrative. Vlad Țepeș. *Vlad the Impaler.*

I thought about a once famous article Ion had written for the international press. Using a pseudonym, Ion had scoffed at the Dictator's most recent campaign to mock America. Taking up the Hollywood portrayal of Dracula as the incarnation of everything demonic and, in the Dictator's mind, therefore assuming that America thought Romania evil, the Dictator wanted to make Vlad the national model. The Dictator proposed that he himself was the latter-day incarnation of the national hero Vlad Țepeș.

The problem with this was that Vlad had been as ruthless to the medieval Romanians as he had been to the Turks, their mortal enemy. Vlad the Impaler was in fact the architect of mass genocide, killing both enemies and his own people. Ion labeled the Dictator "contemporary Romania's supreme hypocrite." The article's brilliant logic was that the *real* Dracula was indeed the Dictator himself. The Dictator styled himself the guardian of all that was good in Romania while "sucking the lifeblood from his own people."

3

Cluj-Napoca, the scenic old Hungarian Transylvanian capital, Hungarian because before Romania had become a country, the region of Transylvania had belonged to Hungary. The hotel faced the broad 14th-century city square, lined with lively shops, cafés, and bookstores. The substantial Roman Catholic Gothic-style church in the middle of the square also signified Cluj's unofficial role as Catholic capital of Romania. The Hungarian-Romanians are Catholic, while virtually all *Romanians* are Eastern Orthodox.

I stood at my hotel window, looking at the pleasant square and picturesque church. I preferred it to Braşov's morose Black Church. I watched some dogs crossing the square, and realized they were everywhere in Romania.

I had unpacked, and was readying to meet my next set of hosts. I looked at the printed itinerary, considering their names. *Mátyás Székely* and *Zsófia Nagy*, and whistled. The first names were tricky enough, but what if I was called on to take a stab at their last names? Then, I realized that my personal linguist would undoubtedly be able to provide a quick lesson in Hungarian pronunciation.

"No idea," Radu said, when I saw him later in the café, where we were to rendezvous with the hosts. He was sitting at a small table, wrapped in his black coat, drinking a Turkish coffee and eating a Danish. Or whatever it was called in Romania. Or Transylvania.

"I never got to Magyar. Now, if their names were Italian …" He chuckled, and asked me if I'd like a coffee.

"Not one of those nasty Turkish things," I said. I realized I had become comfortable with Radu. We were becoming friends enough for me to speak a little sarcastically and honestly with him.

He laughed again. "*Sì*, they are-uh that," he said in a preposterous, pitch-perfect Italian American movie accent. "So, so eh-nasty." He took a sip of the thick black sludge with a grin, and said, "*Molto bene! Molto bene!*" Now more than ever he reminded me of Ion.

This kind of badinage went on while I had a café crème, and then Mr. Székely and Mrs. Nagy appeared. Handshakes all around.

I wasted no time with the name issue. Apologizing and saying I wasn't familiar with Hungarian pronunciation, I asked if they could possibly teach me how to pronounce their names.

And I laughed.

The two Hungarian-Romanians seemed momentarily to be a little stunned.

"Don't worry," Mrs. Nagy said, "just call me Sophie."

"And I'm Matt," Mr. Székely said. "We both spend a lot of time in the UK, so we have our English names. Nobody there would be able to pronounce our Hungarian names."

I was taken to the Transylvanian national museum for my talk. The extraordinarily ornate site cut quite a contrast with the up-to-date ski resort in Braşov. Again, about thirty people sat, this time in a large Rococo room, watching me impassively as I walked in with Radu and my hosts.

I gave the same talk that I had given in Braşov, this time Radu and I playing up the bit with the chemistry vocabulary, and again to good laughs. The Q&A was more of the intellectual class this time, as the audience seemed to be made up of academics, teachers, and a journalist or two.

I got an interesting question from a trim, distinguished-looking woman in a smart suit regarding how I had become interested in writing about food. The woman looked familiar to me, but I couldn't quite place her.

"Food in the States wasn't terribly exciting when I was young, especially in the interior where seasonal produce was limited and people tended to cook the living daylights out of vegetables," I said. "Americans outside of ethnic neighborhoods in the big cities and coasts had little sense of the diversity of ethnic cuisine. 'Mexican' food eaten by Anglos was browned ground beef in a hard taco shell with some cheese and iceberg lettuce. Chinese food was Americanized, which usually meant the spice tamed and some cloyingly sweet sauce added.

"Working mothers made a lot of stews and casseroles to satisfy hungry families, stretch dollars and cut down on prep time during the week. I'm not saying that the food I grew up with wasn't good. It was hearty and flavorful. My mother was a wonderful cook whose parents had been cooks and restaurateurs, but that era of American food often lacked color and … and lightness, and finesse. So I guess the desire came first from realizing what I'd been missing as I encountered the great cuisines of the world, and then curiosity."

At the reception, the slender, smart-looking woman who had asked the interesting question came up with a copy of the Romanian translation of the book, and asked for an autograph. I noted the stylish powder gray gloves, since few women wore gloves anymore except when outside. She said, "I was genuinely interested in hearing you answer the question I asked, but I also wanted to break the ice, so to speak, so that I could talk to you."

I was pleased, and invited the woman, who was named Anca, to join us in a glass of wine. I said that our party would be having dinner soon, and we all could meet after that. We agreed to meet her later at a wine bar that was known to Anca and my hosts. Something about Anca definitely seemed familiar, and it nagged at me that I couldn't place her.

Sophie and Matt took Radu and me to a restaurant near the city square. It was a remarkable place, with foot-thick stone walls and decorated with medieval paraphernalia. While waiting to be seated, Matt and Sophie explained that it was the oldest restaurant in Cluj, once the residence of the Hungarian monarch Matthias Corvinus, who had ruled Transylvania during the 15th century.

The Hungarian king had actually used the residence to

imprison Vlad Ţepeş, the unruly prince. I looked around the restaurant, imagining this medieval scene, the wicked, mad Vlad the Impaler detained in the densely walled structure. Once a poky, now a popular eatery.

While being ushered to our table, Matt said he hoped that I wouldn't mind but he had taken the liberty to invite a French professor who was visiting Cluj. The man had told Matt that he spoke English and would be delighted to meet the famous American writer. Matt thought I might find the professor, who taught at the Sorbonne, interesting.

When we got to our table, we discovered the little French professor sitting there already, before him a nearly empty bottle of wine. And the man didn't really speak English. He appeared to know less English than I know of French.

What's more, he was thoroughly plastered.

As the animated party talked about my talk, the French professor sat silently, drinking the remainder of his bottle.

This was one of those established Romanian restaurants that have wine waiters. He is not a sommelier, as he is an attendant whose sole job is to pour wine. The idea evidently being that the job must be done in an unobtrusive manner, the wine waiter appears and silently pours your glass of wine. The customer is discouraged from pouring his or her own wine, even when it's sitting in front of you on your table. The wine waiter can become offended if you pour it yourself! I don't know whether the communists started this—"when at least everyone had a job"—or if it went back to Vlad's time. Or even Ovid's, for that matter.

The wine waiter appeared with a new bottle of wine, the same label and vintage as the one we had been drinking from, again, the exquisite Saturnalia and its distinctive *terroir*. Utterly silent and looking only at the bottle and wineglass, he gave each of us a fresh pour, completing each dispensation with a flourish, a flick of the wrist.

When he got to the Sorbonne professor, the little man insisted that his empty wineglass be replaced by a clean one. He said that this is done even when one is being poured the same vintage that one has been drinking. He talked about this somewhat at length in his fractured English. Everything he said had to be translated into genuine English for me. I was going to say to him that it would be fine if he just spoke in French, but the man was holding forth.

The waiter didn't seem to understand, so didn't pour the man anything and walked away.

I'd never heard of having your wineglass replaced every time you're poured a glass from a new bottle, but I understood the man to say that this was the universal practice of French wine buffs. I'd spent quite a bit of time in France, among wine devotees, but had never heard of such a severe cultural custom.

Smiling, I told the table that for wine tastings in California you could request a fresh glass when moving from whites to reds, say, but that that was usually about it as far as changing glasses went. I smiled at the little man while Radu translated my remarks into elegant French.

The little professor stormed in response that France's wine tradition was completely different than *California's*! The French had a genuine viticulture, while California simply grew grapes and made middling wine.

Our waiter came with the hors d'oeuvre.

His glass empty, the smashed French professor held his glass out parallel to the table, threatening to drop it on the stone floor if he didn't receive a fresh glass *tout de suite*!

Everyone at the table beseeched him not to dash the glass on the floor! Meanwhile, the alarmed waiter had gone running for the headwaiter, who immediately rushed into the dining room to find out what was going on.

The French professor stood up unsteadily and wanted to give a lecture about viticulture in France, and how important it was for people like Romanians *and Californians* to learn about the proper ways of doing things, all the while holding his wineglass out parallel, ready to drop it. Everyone at the table implored him to sit down. He stood there for a minute or two, intoning about wines and the right way of doing things. Then suddenly he sat down, abruptly dozing in his chair, the empty glass unsmashed before him.

After dinner, our entourage found Anca in a chic wine bar on the square. Following a few glasses of wine, Sophie, Matt, and Radu excused themselves for the evening. My hotel was across the square, so I could find my way back unaccompanied.

The woman's gloves now removed, I immediately realized that Anca was in fact the same woman I had sat next to on the plane, the one with the scar on her right hand. But I didn't say anything about this. Surely, it must be a coincidence.

But it wasn't. We engaged in some small talk, and then Anca looked at me closely and said, "I saw you on the plane from Paris to Otopeni," the Bucharest airport. "And then I saw the photo of you in the newspaper, saying you would be speaking here in Cluj."

Spellbound by this woman, I listened intently.

"Coming back to Romania has been a kind a homecoming for me. I have been living in Paris for a number of years, a refugee from the old regime. I am here in Cluj to visit old friends. I am originally from Sinaia, and I have returned to claim some family property that the old government took and gave to others. Now a new law makes it possible for me to reclaim the family property, but it is a time-consuming process. I have not decided yet whether to return to France and resume my now settled life there, or to try to make a go of staying in Romania. I am not sure I want to be a Romanian anymore."

The scarred hand held the glass of blood-red wine. I took in the wound in such a way that I hoped Anca didn't see me looking at it. The disfigurement spanned the entire top of the hand, slanting across the veins, a ghastly dark line that seemed not to have ever quite healed.

I asked Anca what she had done in the past, before she had left Romania.

"I was a high school French teacher," Anca said. "I taught at the French school here. I was married." She didn't elaborate on what had transpired.

I tried to imagine what it must feel like to be returning under such circumstances. I was also returning under a complex state of affairs, but of course the situation wasn't remotely similar. I'd wanted to see Ion and I'd wanted to experience Romania again, to recollect some of that inexplicable feeling I'd had during the bad old time, when I was young and bold, and—feeling guilty about it—had had *a grand old time*.

I decided on what I thought was a safe question. I asked how Anca had learned English so well. "You speak it like a native."

Anca said, "I don't, really. But I lived in London for some time, before settling in Paris. Like many Romanians, I have a gift for language. I was a refugee, with no money and no job and no … what do you say, *resources*. Then I got a translating job in Paris, translating Romanian." This made her smile sardonically. "You see? I went from being a French teacher in Romania to a Romanian translator in France. My life was upside down."

Anca made no mention of her husband, so I assumed he must not have been able to accompany her to the UK and France. I felt sad for Anca, and wanted to help in some way. But

I couldn't think of anything.

"I was also here in Romania before the Revolution," I said.

Anca looked surprised and interested. "How so?"

"Oh, I was here on a government grant, but really just traveling around, footloose and still relatively young. I met a wonderful man, someone I'm sure you've heard of. Ion Vadim, the Minister of Education. I met him after he'd been released from prison, after the treason charge was finally dropped."

Anca listened as I spoke, looking impressed.

"You know about him?" I asked, pleased.

"Yes, of course I know about him. Everyone my age does."

That night I dreamed about Anca. Ion was in the dream, too. Anca and Ion acted like they didn't know one another, but I could tell they did. Anca seemed to be in distress. Finally, troubled, I asked Ion about this. He said, "We are Romanian. We all know one another. We always have. You wouldn't understand."

You wouldn't understand.

I awoke, unaware of where I was. I looked around the hotel room, and realized I was still in Cluj. And then the dream came back to me, and I wondered what it meant.

Radu knocked at the door, saying we were running late for the train to Sibiu.

I joined him downstairs at the café where we had met Sophie and Matt. Radu was drinking a café crème. I had a Danish and washed it down with two strong coffees. I told Radu about the scar on Anca's hand.

"How terrible," he said. He considered his own hands, the same shade as his café crème, perhaps imagining what it would be like to be stigmatized in such a way.

I related the patchy story that Anca had told me. Radu said, "There are many stories like this from the old days. Our parents starved while the Dictator paid off the national debt, and he and his family lived like tzars." He looked around the café at the young people, professionals and hipsters mixed together. "My generation has its own problems, but nothing like our parents'."

Both Radu and I were unusually quiet on the train ride to Sibiu. I kept thinking about Anca. In fact, everyone in their car seemed subdued, silently staring out the windows at the passing landscape.

You wouldn't understand.

4

Sibiu was another spectacular Transylvanian city set against stately mountains. The city center was being torn apart as part of a massive reconstruction plan. The city had had a streetcar system, scotched for some reason by the communists, and now being restored. Getting around the city was difficult. I felt tired from the traveling and moving.

The hotel was another flamboyant Rococo structure, with warm rooms and a dining hall. Radu and I met our Sibiu hosts, who evidently couldn't speak any English at all. As a result, the conversation was a bit strained and laborious. Despite an attempt to retain their names, I couldn't hang on to them in my mind. I was bushed.

I felt bad about all this, being unable to speak Romanian, being unable to retain the hosts' names. I just don't have the gift for languages, and when I can't converse directly with someone, I find it hard to connect.

My talk at the Sibiu museum, however, brought in a considerably larger group than before. Surprised, I estimated that several hundred souls occupied the seats, and more stood and sat where they could. It was standing room only. Numbers lined the walls, leaning against pillars, sitting on steps. Even more astonishing, when I entered, the room erupted in applause. Everyone sitting stood up to give me an ovation!

I was taken aback by this, and bowed a little, smiling uncertainly. I looked at Radu, who now stood beside me. He grinned and shrugged, holding his hands palms up.

"They must have me confused with someone else," I murmured to him.

I gave the same talk as before, but this time I was interrupted several times by more eager applause after Radu had translated something. I had no idea what was going on.

During the Q&A afterward, a young woman asked me what it was like to be a famous writer.

I laughed my unique laugh. And this seemed to please the crowd immensely. People turned in their seats to lightly punch each other, laughing.

What the heck!

"I'm not famous," I said. "I'm lucky enough to be able to make my living as a writer. Aside from some brief jobs when I was young, I've never actually done anything else. But I'm not famous."

The assembly seemed unconvinced. Again, they turned to one another, smiling as if in acknowledgment of something.

A man rose and asked a very peculiar question: "Where did your laugh come from?"

I was sure it must be some kind of mistake. I made Radu repeat the translated question. The audience members who apparently understood English laughed when they heard me ask that the question be clarified, and the rest laughed when they heard Radu repeat his translation.

Where did my laugh come from?

I'd never thought about it before. I knew that some people

thought I had a voluble, curious laugh, and that some thought my laugh was obnoxious—well, a man I'd dated for a while, anyway. But did it come from somewhere?

"My mother," I said, realizing it for the first time. I thought about my late Greek-American mother, who had started as a waitress in a restaurant my father owned, and went on to become a grand cook. I thought of the food. I thought of my mother's laugh, how strangers would step away in alarm, but it was the thing that made my English Jewish father fall in love with her. That laugh was a deeply happy, mirthful response to the sometimes difficult, *meshuggah* world.

5

It was my turn to doze on the three-hour train ride back to Bucharest. By the time Radu and I arrived, it was cold and dark, and I was ready for dinner and bed. The Romani women and their children saw me, and I gave them some paper lei, smiling to show that I couldn't speak Romanian.

I asked Radu if he would like one for the road. The hotel had a pleasant, quiet bar. I was being polite.

Radu looked very tired, as well, and apologized, saying he had to be getting home. He stood outside the doors of the hotel in the cold, looking at the warm taxis idling in a neat row. The Romani women and children watched him.

"You know," he said, "I may take a taxi home. It has been a long day."

"You should! It's so cold now, and if you take the metro— though obviously superior to London, Paris, and New York's— you won't get home till late."

Radu looked me, and laughed a little at my teasing. I thought of suggesting I be permitted to pay for his cab fare, but thought better before saying so. I knew that Radu would rather walk home than take money from me for a cab. I thought he was just like Ion had been, back in the bad old days.

PART III

1

I rose fairly late on the day I was set for my special Bucharest talk. The Transylvanian tour had left me feeling fatigued, so I went about getting into the day in a leisurely way. I was looking forward to seeing *Last Supper* in person for the first time, finally, and soaking up the feeling of the Cozma Cabinet. I looked forward to seeing Ion again even more.

I thought of my return to Romania as one of the best episodes in my life thus far.

Before Radu was scheduled to pick me up, I took a stroll around the bustling city center area, with a mind toward having lunch. It was my first chance to wander around the lively governmental and business district in daylight. When I had seen it last, it was far from being full of life. It had been a nearly deserted, dirty gray urban wasteland, beautiful old interwar period buildings being demolished and in their place hideous concrete blocks being erected.

Nevertheless, I had fond memories of it, all of them associated with Ion. I noted how prosperous the city now looked. Stores with stylish clothing, storerooms with elegant furnishings, large stores vending gleaming appliances.

As I walked along, looking for a suitable place to have lunch, I began to notice a singular occurrence. Passersby were talking in Romanian, and then suddenly would erupt in a sort of loud, bizarre hiccupping noise. And then others near this person, even strangers passing the other way, it seemed, would laugh and echo the sound.

"HA! HA! HA!"

I stopped and stood in the street, bewildered by this. If I had encountered it once, I would have thought it simply one of those baffling things one experiences a single time while in another country. But it occurred several times.

And then one of the passersby, a young man, looked at me, his eyes widening, and pointed at me. He then barked with what seemed to be delight, and said something rapidly in Romanian. Soon a small crowd had surrounded me, all of them making that stupefying noise and pointing at me!

"HA! HA! HA!"

Pursued by the merry mob, I ducked into a café and found a table in the back, my back to the wall. I sat there, perspiring a little, trying to understand what had just happened when a grinning young woman came over and spoke to me. I said in my best Romanian that I would like a café crème. The woman looked confused and said something in Romanian. I watched the woman walk over to a table and sit down.

Eventually, another young woman came over, and I realized that this one was the actual waitperson, because I understood the woman to be asking me what I wanted.

I tried my Romanian again, and it was understood.

I sat there a bit stunned, trying to comprehend what had just taken place with the first young woman, who now sat gawping at me from her table across the room. I would have gotten up and spoken to the woman, except for the obvious and insurmountable obstacle to communication. My inability to speak the language was especially galling, as this seemed like some bizarre misunderstanding that I could easily rectify.

Abruptly, the mysterious young woman stood up and pointed at me, saying,

"HA! HA! HA!"

I gaped back at her, utterly mystified. The woman left the café.

If I hadn't heard others in the street doing the same thing, I would have assumed that the poor woman had some sort of pitiable neurological problem. But what could it possibly be? It was exactly the same behavior as I'd encountered in the street.

I drank my coffee and left.

In the street, I continued to hear it.

"HA! HA! HA!"

I was beginning to feel alarmed, as if I was the subject of some vast conspiracy. As if everyone around me knew some secret about me that even I didn't know. I hurried back to the hotel. I didn't want to see any strangers, and even took the stairs to my fourth floor room. I didn't want to take the chance of being trapped with some nut-job Romanian on the elevator!

Once in the room, I called room service and had an omelet sent up. I sat on the bed, laptop open, cell phone out, drinking directly from the peewee wine bottle obtained from the mini-bar, slowly eating my omelet, and puzzling out what had just transpired. I could come up with no sane explanation for any of it!

When I turned on the TV, I was greeted with the Gypsy rap music show. This is one strange country, I thought.

2

Radu's email message said he would pick me up at 16:00—Right, I thought, that's 4 o'clock—and that he had some "very weird news" for me. I stared at the message, wondering what this very weird news could be. I'd had enough mystery for one day. Not only that, but I had a headache and had noticed through the day more and more congestion in my head until it felt like it was stuffed full of mucus.

"Crap. Sinus infection. Cold. The *curent*. Whatever it is, this is not a good time. Just before the most challenging talk."

It was typical, though. Traveling has always worn me down, and I often get whatever is going around. I made sure to stuff my bag full of tissues, and stopped in at the hotel shop for throat lozenges.

"You're not going to believe it," Radu said, when he saw me in the lobby. He looked very excited. Beaming at me, he was almost dancing in place.

"Look, I've had a strange day so far, *and* I'm coming down with the plague, so let's get to the point, already," I said, exasperated. "What's this *weird news* you have for me?"

Just then, a dignified-looking middle-aged man in a tailored business suit walked by, paused, looked at me, and …

"HA! HA! HA!"

The man chuckled and walked on, as if hurrying to an important meeting.

I turned to Radu and said, "That exact same thing happened earlier today! I was out, having a walk, and people all over the place were making that bizarre noise. Some of them surrounded me and started doing it while pointing at me. They chased me into a café, where a woman did the same freaking thing! *What the hell is going on?*"

Radu, too excited to acknowledge my bout of uncharacteristic ill temper, was shaking his head and smiling through all this, both hands up in a sign of reassurance.

He said, "You are famous! You are an instant celebrity here!"

My mind went back to the bewildering experience in Sibiu, when the audience had behaved so oddly.

"But how?" I asked.

"The TV interview," Radu said. "You became a national sensation while we were traveling around Transylvania. I would have figured out what was going on in Sibiu, but didn't have the time. I was busy with work I'd taken with me."

"But the bizarre noise! What the *hell* is that?"

Radu was grinning. He said, "It's your laugh. Your wonderful laugh. The interview was a big sensation. Everyone seems to have seen it. And TV shows here get replayed, so the people who didn't see it the first time knew to watch it when it came on again. People all over Romania saw it. They loved what you said about Romanian food, and they loved the way you handled that arrogant host. But most of all, they loved your laugh."

That caught me off guard. My laugh?

"I know it's a funny laugh. Friends have told me that. But it's not that strange."

Radu said, "Vita, your laugh is incredible. People all over Romania are saying that it's a great joy to hear. I think we Romanians needed something like this. We're going through tough times, and we needed something to make us feel united as a nation."

I stood there, trying to take it all in. Years ago I'd said I wanted to be famous, when I was young, had published my first book, and was audacious enough to imagine myself a celebrated author. But it just hadn't happened. And I'd gotten used to the idea that I would never achieve that level of success. Yet, here I was in Bucharest, Romania, a place I had come back to largely out of a hope to rekindle that once burning love for Ion, and I had become famous overnight. Hah.

"I don't believe it," I said. "It's just a curious, one-day thing, like a passing stomach bug. It won't even amount to a blip or a hiccup. Whatever it is, it'll be over in a day or two."

Radu drove me to the National Gallery, where I was to give my talk. Long lines snaked outside in the cold.

"Oh, my God," Radu said. "Oh, my God."

"What's going on? They must all be here for the special new Cozma exhibit. Right?"

Radu said, "They're waiting for you, Vita. They're here to see you!"

I protested. This couldn't possibly be why hundreds of people waited in line to get into a museum.

Radu spent some time looking for a parking space, and we ended up more than a block from the museum.

Sure enough, as we made our way to the museum's front doors, the people waiting in line spotted me and erupted in applause and cheers, waving and beaming at me. Nearly all carried Romanian copies of *Snouts, Tails, Entrails*.

"This is so strange," I said. "I don't feel myself at all!"

A number of people howled above the rest, "HA! HA! HA!"

I couldn't help shrinking from the scene. I tentatively waved back, then hurried through the doors.

Inside, just past the front doors of the museum, Ana, Madga, and Mihai were waiting for us. Ana said, "You are an instant phenomenon. It's amazing, isn't it?" Her eyes wide, she seemed pleased yet somewhat distressed by the mob outside.

I nodded and agreed that it was certainly amazing, then took out a tissue and blew my nose. The three looked at me sympathetically, turned to each other and said, "The *curent*."

Ana said, "Let's go to the Cozma Cabinet. Ms. Codreanu, the director, is there, so you can meet her. The American Ambassador is also there!"

"The American Ambassador? Why?"

"You're a sensation," Magda said. "A famous American writer giving a very popular talk in the capital."

But first Ana wanted to make a brief stop at her office to grab something. The office was full of Cozma archival materials, spilling out of their marked boxes. Documents, photographs, curious drawings were strewn across her desk, on the floor, on the shelves. Ana picked up her notebook and looked at it. "My notes on the exhibit," she said. "I just wanted to check something."

When we reached the room being called the Cozma Cabinet, I was happy and relieved to see Ion standing just outside the door, talking to the director, as he had a way of making me feel calm. I hadn't been sure how, or whether, we'd be able to connect in such chaotic circumstances. He caught my eye and grinned appealingly.

The others might have noticed that our greeting kiss wasn't that characteristically Romanian left-right pecks on the cheeks of friends, but I didn't care. Let them look.

"Ms. Codreanu and I are old friends," Ion said. "I called her when I saw the mobs outside, and she let me in by the side door."

Ana introduced me to Ms. Codreanu, who welcomed me to the museum, saying she was delighted to have a writer of my "distinction" giving a talk that was associated with the opening of the Cozma special exhibit. I almost said, "What distinction? That people think I have a weird laugh?" But I held my tongue.

Ms. Codreanu then introduced me to the American Ambassador. The Hon. Mr. John Phelps looked just like an American ambassador should look. Tall, lean, a full head of white hair, and in a fine suit. But not quite as tall as me.

"I'm honored to meet you, Ms. Unwin," the Ambassador said. "We don't get a lot of eminent American authors who become an instant hit in Romania."

Everyone except me chuckled for a moment.

I said, "Thank you, Mr. Ambassador, but I'm not an eminent writer. But I guess I am a hit in Romania."

Everyone laughed a little more loudly this time. I decided to try not to laugh for the evening. My laugh had caused enough bother.

The Ambassador said that his wife was very sorry that she couldn't be there, that she was "a big fan." He then passed me his professional card, and said that if there was anything I needed while in country, I should contact him. On the back a phone number was handwritten.

He said, "I've written my personal cell number on the back. Call, please, before you leave the country. My wife very much wants to meet you."

Ion took my arm, and I stuck the card in my pocket and forgot about it.

We walked into the small but well-filled room together, and I glanced around, taking in what I considered the more minor stuff. A glass-topped case with some of Cozma's sketches set against a wall. Several of his smaller pieces, disturbing-looking sculptures that seemed to represent truncated parts of a human body sat under Plexiglas cubes.

But *Last Supper*. As I walked toward it I felt as in a dream. There it stood in the middle of the room in all its raw, gory massiveness, the real piece assaulting my eyes. In spite of my years looking at and studying the photos, I hadn't been prepared for its shocking power. It was a solid, heavy piece, larger than I'd expected. More menacing-looking than in the photos. Maybe it was the light of the room, spots directed at the sculpture from all directions, the other pieces much more subtly lit.

The room's lighting gave a surreal quality to the experience of seeing the art works. Ana and the other staff had created something powerful here.

At one end of the room stood a table covered with a white cloth, with wine bottles and platters of fruits and cheese on top, along with a coffee urn and demitasse cups. The reception table.

Mihai offered to get me some coffee, and I told him I could use a jolt of the black stuff.

Damn, I was exhausted. The stupid sinus thing, the touring, the night of bad sleep. I leaned a little on Ion. The others noticed this.

The Director cleared her throat and said, "There's been a change of plan. I'm afraid we can't bring so many people into the Cozma Cabinet. But we have a solution. We've decided to put you in the museum auditorium. It's much bigger than the Cabinet."

"Not talk in here? But my talk is specifically designed for the setting! And what about the projector? I have images to show."

I was disappointed and didn't care if I showed it. It had been the only thing keeping me going.

"It's a shame about not being able to do your talk in the Cozma Cabinet," Magda said, "but you are now a famous personality in Romania. That's nice, isn't it? And Ms. Codreanu is making sure that you can use the large projector and screen in the auditorium."

It did seem like the only solution.

I took the demitasse Mihai handed me and took a tentative sip. He had put a good tablespoon of sugar in it. I almost choked and put it down on the white tablecloth.

Ion said, "It's going to be brilliant. You're going to be brilliant." He smiled his most disarming smile, which reassured me somewhat. Really, though I'd hesitate to tell anyone this, I have a bit of stage fright. With a small crowd, I can make eye contact with people, connect with them. But an auditorium sounded vast and impersonal.

We entered the auditorium through the back doors, and I could see that it had a capacity of a few hundred. Yet every inch was occupied—seats, floors, and steps. They were all there to hear me talk about offal. And of course to hear my "distinctive" laugh.

Ana, Magda, and Radu walked with me toward the stage, while Mihai, the Ambassador, and Ms. Codreanu went to their reserved seats in front. I'd wanted Ion to stay near, just offstage, but we saw that there was no good vantage point, so he sweetly volunteered to muddle through the crowd and watch like everyone else. He promised to keep his eyes on me, to reassure me. Squeezed my hand and went to the back, where he found some standing room.

As we stepped on stage, the crowd broke out with applause and rooting, many chanting, "HA! HA! HA!"

Well, what to do but make the best of it? I smiled the most convincing smile I could, turned to Radu beside me and asked, "Is this safe? The only exit is completely blocked."

Radu shrugged. "This is Romania." I saw that perspiration had broken out on his forehead.

The crowd was noisy and a bit unruly. People were chattering and laughing.

Ana turned on the sizeable ceiling projector, which needed to warm up, and then brought down the large, electronically controlled video screen. She loaded my presentation disk into the computer unit, and then handed me the remote.

The screen gradually lit up, illuminating the first image, a simple white background with black letters: "Inside Cozma's Cabinet: Offal in *Last Supper*."

Before the auditorium lights went down, to my relief I was able to make out several familiar faces in the audience. Dick Elbow, wearing a suit, was sitting in front next to Ms. Codreanu and Mihai. He gestured to me as I caught his eye. On the edge was the know-it-all American, whose name escaped me. I spotted Ştefania Popescu, one of my hosts in Braşov, sitting a few rows back, and not far from her, my Cluj hosts, Sophie and Matt, the Hungarian-Romanians, who gave me a little wave. Sophie was sitting next to the Ambassador. They were talking. When I saw Anca—standing in the aisle, again wearing her gray gloves—it was somehow not surprising. I guess I really was a sensation, at least the sensation of the hour.

Then I caught sight of Ion standing in the back of the auditorium, his head plainly visible above those of the other men. I smiled and waved at him, and he gestured in return. Knowing where he was made me feel better, more relaxed, less sick. Even happy.

Then Ana, standing by the door, dimmed the auditorium lights. It was now dark, impossible to make out any of the faces in the audience.

Magda, the outgoing young art professor, introduced me. She walked out on the stage, stepping into a pool of light. The mass began to quiet down, and then was silent, watching her.

Radu whispered the translation into English as Magda introduced herself, telling the throng that it was her distinct pleasure to welcome America's most famous food writer, Ms. Vita Unwin. The crowd cheered and clapped for several protracted seconds. Magda listed the titles of my books in Romanian, and when she got to *Snouts, Tails, Entrails*, the mob broke out again in wild applause.

Magda also noted that I'd captivated Romanians on a recent cultural talk show, and that I was categorically *not* a cookbook writer!

The crowd went wild, with deafening hoots of "HA! HA! HA!"

They continued chanting this, and showed no sign of stopping! The din was even weirder in the dark than it had been in the light.

I grabbed Radu's hand, and we walked onto the dais—to even louder cheers. I thanked Magda for the flattering introduction, and gave the young professor a hug, then turned toward the audience. I held up my hands, and the mob quieted immediately.

I'd never felt that kind of power before in my life! Maybe I could get used to fame.

"I'm honored and very pleased that you have come out in such numbers. I hope that my talk today pleases you as much as my TV appearance apparently did."

Radu translated the comment, which drew more of the same applause and appreciation.

Then I launched into my lecture, starting off with an expression of regret that the talk could not have taken place in the Cozma Cabinet, as planned, because I was going to address my remarks to a fantastic work of art recently brought to light and now available for display, titled *Last Supper*.

As I got caught up in the rhythm of my talk, I forgot about the large crowd and the symptoms of my sinus infection and my voice gained strength. This was going to work.

I talked of how critics put Cozma's art in the company of Francis Bacon, Lucian Freud, and other artists of the post-apocalyptic grotesque. The difference being that, as a Romanian, Cozma was much more political in intent, and the content of his works overtly expressed his political temper. I added that, of course, Romanians best knew Cozma's art, so I wasn't saying anything new about that. I remarked that over the years a few people who knew Cozma personally had written in correspondence of the obscure sculpture, *Last Supper*, saying it was simultaneously breathtaking, disconcerting, and inspiring.

I clicked the remote and the next image appeared, a comprehensive anterior shot of *Last Supper*, thirteen figures at a table, eating a meal. Some in the crowd gasped at the sight of the entire art piece, and I could tell that many turned to their neighbors to whisper something. Most went silent.

"My focus is on the portrayal of the food being devoured in the sculpture. Devoured," I said, "is the appropriate word for it."

"Clearly, it is not food that appears in Renaissance portrayals of Christ's Last Supper, and it is not food that would have been served in the period and geographical location of Christ's time." I brought up the next two images, Leonardo's and then Tintoretto's *The Last Supper*. "Let's note that Cozma's title was *Last Supper*, not 'The' Last Supper. Did he mean to indicate a timelessness about this portrayal of a last supper?"

The food shown in the sculpture was plainly Romanian "peasant" fare. I brought up the next image from the sculpture, a close-up of the *drob de miel*. Cozma's rendition of the dish was precise, and some of the audience murmured, I assumed, in recognition of it. I explained that English-speakers recognize this dish as haggis, a Scottish recipe made with heart, liver, and lungs.

Next I showed a close-up of the *sângerete*, or emulsified blood sausage. Then, the artwork's credible realization of *fudulii de porc*, or pork testicles.

Next was an image that focused on the *tobă*, a dish called "headcheese" in English. Finally, I showed *Last Supper*'s grotesque human-animal figures devouring *creier pane*—brains. "Brains and headcheese. As Cozma was an Anglophile, this was likely a sardonic joke on his part. I also would say that Cozma saw these two dishes as related, symbolically."

As Radu translated, the audience grew stony silent. Many Romanians regarded Cozma's art as offensive, though I wouldn't have expected those people to attend the lecture.

Some thought it blatant sacrilege, others were uncomfortable with its open satire of Romanian politics, and still others wanted to put that history behind and move on. The hitherto relatively unknown *Last Supper* was almost certainly his most intentionally monstrous and emotionally taxing work of art.

Then I showed a wide-ranging shot of the back of the three-dimensional sculpture.

"As you can see, the figures in the sculpture have human masks and human clothing, but behind their human masquerade are their true vulture faces. Just as in Renaissance depictions of the Last Supper, there are thirteen figures, and what appears to be a figure that on some level takes the central place of Christ.

"Though, I would point out that there is nothing religious about this sculpture. It has none of the characteristics of sacred art. No lit coronas, no golden dinner service—no sign of inspirational spiritual qualities. It is a murky, disconcerting, grotesque glimpse of something real, and unmistakably meant to convey political symbolism. The figures are political cannibals, devouring the entrails of their countrymen and women, and the viewer is encouraged to guess who each figure represents in Romanian politics.

"Who each one is meant to be, no one has yet determined."

3

When the lights came up, I steeled myself for the onslaught of provocative questions that always seemed to follow my talks in Romania.

A man stood up and took the passed microphone.

"What are your thoughts on the theory that the Dictator is represented by the Judas figure rather than the central figure?

This is a theory among some art scholars, based on a single letter that made its way back to Romania after Cozma's death, but before the current collection. The idea is that Judas is an obvious betrayer of the people, thus the Dictator, but that the central figure—I hesitate to call him even a reference to Christ—is more secretive, less easy to uncover."

It wasn't an entirely unexpected question, but I didn't have much to say.

"It is interesting to speculate, and I hope a puzzle that can be solved some day, maybe once all of the Cozma documents have been cataloged, work that is being done now by several young people, including the scholar who introduced me, and my own incomparable translator." I gestured toward Radu, who bowed to the audience with feigned solemnity. "They will have the answer for you, I suspect. For me, I have only heard the same rumors as you, so I demur to the hard-working scholars."

The man and the crowd both seemed satisfied with the answer.

I answered a few additional, more innocuous questions. Then Ms. Codreanu came up, shook my hand, and formally closed the lecture.

The adrenaline was still pumping through me. I felt like it had gone well, I'd held the large crowd, and now I was free! As I walked off the stage, my other lecture hosts and Anca came up to me. I kissed Ştefania and Matt on the cheek, hesitated a moment, and though she seemed somewhat aloof, went ahead and kissed Anca lightly as well. When you're a guest in a foreign country, everyone you know is a friend.

The Ambassador was standing there, arm in arm with Sophie, both smiling broadly.

Sophie said, "Vita, have you met John Phelps, the American Ambassador?"

"We're old friends, Sophie and I," the Ambassador said. "Whenever my wife and I are in Cluj, we always visit with Sophie and her husband. Fascinating talk!"

"It was thrilling!" Ştefania said, in agreement. The others added similar comments.

"I wasn't sure, at first. I thought the crowd was a bit strange, so quiet."

"Yes, that did seem odd," the Ambassador said. "But the seriousness of the subject, the shocking images, I can understand it."

Toward the back of the auditorium, a knot of humanity was forming, with raised voices. The noise quotient grew rapidly as it seemed like everyone began talking at once.

I turned to the Ambassador. "When I first arrived in Romania I'd thought that conversations had often sounded like arguments, and wondered whether I'd made a mistake coming to stay in such a contentious country. Exasperated, I'd finally asked a Romanian companion what the fight was about. He'd looked confused, then said, 'Oh, they're not fighting, they're having an intellectual discourse about music.'"

Everyone thought this was funny.

"Maybe the raised voices now are having an intellectual discourse about Cozma's work," Sophie said.

Or about my talk.

Radu, looking mystified, appeared at my side to escort me to the invitation-only reception in the Cabinet.

"Why do you think they became so quiet when I brought up the images? Do you think I offended them?" I had to yell above the din.

Radu shook his head and shrugged.

"That seems unlikely. Really unlikely," he yelled back. "Romanians just don't act like that. I don't know what the deal is."

Radu led the way through the tight crowd, politely but firmly pushing between the bodies so densely packed together that they seemed more like a single entity than a grouping of discrete objects.

The rest of the group followed, like a snake slipping between rocks.

The din grew as they approached the auditorium door, people seemed agitated and spoke in louder and louder voices.

"Radu, this has been a very strange day. I'm exhausted and befuddled. What is with the crowd? What the hell is going on?"

He stopped and spoke to one of the men in the crowd. I picked up on the words "*omar*" and "*omucidere.*" Radu said, "They're talking about a death, a murder. Maybe it's death represented by *Last Supper*? Maybe a heart attack? Surely it can't be anything else."

"Oh, I'm certain it's the sculpture they're talking about!"

When we finally made it through the mass, Magda was there, tears streaming. She pulled at Radu's arm, mouthed something to him, and he slumped. From the back he looked like a puppet whose strings had been cut. I instinctively reached out to him, thinking he might fall, and pulled him away from the crowd.

Radu leaned against a wall, head in hands. Magda babbled in an un-Magda-like way. She gestured me toward the Cozma Cabinet.

I felt a catch in my breath, a little skip of fear in my heart. This would be bad, really bad. I didn't want to imagine, so I had to see. I walked through the door and encountered a scene that was viciously violent. On the floor near *Last Supper* lay little Ana, face up, eyes open but empty, what looked like a choker necklace around her neck, a red choker.

Momentarily uncomprehending, I tried to rectify images of

Ana—Ana goofily tipsy on cheap beer, Ana earnest and excited about the donation of the collection, with Ana, supine on the floor, blood beading around her neck, eyes unseeing.

In the background, sirens grew louder. Before the police could take over, with their tape and their restrictions and their questions, I quickly surveyed the room. Ana lay before what must be the display case of Cozma's documents. The glass top of the case had been smashed and the papers within looked rifled through. One of the small but heavy looking Cozma sculptures lay among the papers. Glass shards littered the floor, picking up the light and bouncing it back in an inappropriately festive way. Glass bits sparkled on Ana's face.

The table covered with a white cloth, with opened wine bottles and platters of fruits and cheese on top, was undisturbed.

Last Supper also stood undisturbed, though now even more disturbing than before: the garish colors, the grotesque faces under the masks. The central figure with his hand upturned and blood on the palm.

Now there were two competing violences in the room: the sculpture and the real human body. Much as I care about art, it isn't life. This was life, violently snuffed out.

The hairless American guy showed up, shouting, "Everyone stand back! The police will be here momentarily. Do not touch anything!"

I looked at the fool. What was he doing here?

The police arrived and started ordering people here and there, breaking up the gawking crowd, securing the space.

I searched for Radu, but couldn't spot him anywhere.

Then someone tapped me on the shoulder. I turned to face Dick Elbow. "You must leave now, Ms. Unwin. You must go now." He was speaking in a low voice, hard for me to understand among the noise.

"What? What do you mean? My friend Ana has been murdered. It's terrible!"

"Yes, it's terrible," he said, "and you must leave right away and not get involved. As your US representative in Romania, I am telling you you must leave *now*."

Ion appeared, and I felt a huge sense of relief—someone to share this horror with. Someone to help. Ion said to Elbow, "I can get Vita out of here."

Elbow looked at Ion curiously, then nodded. "Of course, Mr. Vadim. Your help is appreciated."

I felt shaky, so held onto Ion's arm. "Radu has to be insane right now. I should find him."

Ion said no. So like him just to say it so plainly.

"His friends will take care of him. You need to get out of here. Come back to my place. We can decide what to do after you have hot bath and a drink. Your head will be clearer then."

It was a relief to give up my will for a moment, so I let Ion lead me.

Then in the car tears started.

"It's not that I knew her very well. Only met her a couple of times. But she was a good kid, a sweet girl, and I know Radu was in love with her. And it was so ugly. And she was so happy before, seeing the big crowd. Who? What, what kind of freak …?"

"No doubt some freak, as you say. Maybe the violence of the art piece set him off. Who knows with murderers. The police will sort it out. Poor girl. And her poor friends."

In the apartment, I forced down one of the sandwiches Ion had ordered, though the drink went down easily. The first one, and the second. After a bath, third drink in hand, I lay on the sofa with my head in Ion's lap.

"Let me take you away, Vita. The Consulate will understand. I'll speak to Elbow. He can rearrange things. You need a rest. Tomorrow, we can go to my country house. It's quiet. It's beautiful there. We'll have everything we need."

4

Ion drove us himself this time. He popped a disc into the player. Satie's "Gymnopédie No. 1" came on. The soothing piano piece was a good one to calm frazzled nerves.

The roads were uncrowded, and better than I'd remembered. Money had been spent.

"Tell me about your house. I want to hear something nice and good. Something that has nothing to do with art or food or death."

"It belonged to my grandparents," he said. "We got it back after the Dictator's ouster, though it was in poor shape. It was built to resemble a French stone farmhouse, with large, sunny rooms, a stream view, and extensive gardens. I've been working on it for years now, but I love working on it. It's fortifying and satisfying to see the progress you've made bit by bit."

The countryside rolled past, getting lusher and hillier the farther we got from the city. We'd be in the tall pines soon, near the ski resort town of Sinaia. As we drove, I could feel my chest untightening, my sinuses unstuffing.

"Do you think it's really true? About the ill health effects of living in the city?"

"Yes, of course," Ion answered. "The air can be foul: too many cars now. Too many delivery trucks. Romania is very behind the times in controlling pollution. It's like any city, with good and bad. You will feel the difference here. I know I can run farther and breathe easier in the mountains. There's a mineral spring nearby we could bathe in, too. It's excellent for the body."

"Do you believe in the *curent?*" I asked after a short pause.

Ion laughed.

"I'm a modern person, Vita. I'm of the next generation. We can laugh at the childish beliefs of the past. I like to open windows, when I'm out of the city where the air is fresh. I wonder how much the illnesses from the *draft* are really due to the polluted air."

"Mmmm." I was only half listening. I was feeling myself unwind. It had been horrible, horrible. It's not that I could get the horrific picture out of my mind, but that I felt more relaxed, more able to let my mind wander over the details and to think.

"What do you think? About the murder, I mean," I asked. "Ana certainly didn't seem like someone who could possibly have enemies. It looks like something else was going on, and I don't really believe it could be a psycho. Too pat. It looked desperate and sudden. Maybe something to do with the Cabinet."

Ion made a noise that suggested he was thinking about it.

"Are you sure you want to get into this morbid subject? I thought we were getting away from that," he said.

"I can't not think. I have to think about it. I notice things, you know. I close my eyes and I see the whole scene. No mess at all except for the broken glass. It must have been quick, as I didn't see any sign of struggle. Of course, that could also mean it was someone she knew so she wasn't prepared. How can someone be prepared? I mean, oh, I feel like I'm being callous conjecturing like this. Yes, let's drop the subject for a while. I want to just be with you."

"You simply should not think about it anymore," Ion said.

"It will make you feel ill."

We pulled down a long, stone drive that wound through tall pines and ended in a loop in the center of which was a fountain and benches. To the right was a garden that appeared to wrap around the back, full of flowers in raised beds, plants of varied heights, what looked like a limestone patio with a table and cushioned chairs that bespoke late, lazy mornings with a newspaper and coffee.

Then, through an arched door of weathered wood, I stepped into a lovely, soothing space, all in pale blues and blue-grays, with comfortable furnishings, light curtains pulled open, a fireplace ready to light. Ion showed me through to the back of the house, where a sitting room was bathed in sunlight and on an ottoman sat a copper tray laden with pastries and a decanter of liquor of some kind, cognac maybe.

"I had the housekeeper make it ready for us," Ion said. "I do come up here when I can, but that's not often enough. I have a small staff, an old couple, that lives on the property, close enough to get here in minutes, but not so close that I feel crowded. They care for the gardens and clean, and cook when I'm in, but it needed airing out and provisioning. There is no sense keeping food here that will go bad."

"This is so different from your apartment in the city! But I think I can see it, a need for solitude at times, the lure of the woods. It is very much a retreat from the world. I wonder if you'd be surprised by my modern house with its streamlined, simple geometry and walls of glass."

"Of course! Everything about you is surprising, and at the same time reassuring and familiar. Familiar because of our past, I suppose. Surprising because I don't think I could have predicted the shape your life would take back when you, we, were so young. I did think you might make something of yourself, though it was never a sure thing."

He motioned me to a leather armchair, into which I sank, kicked off my shoes, and stretched my long legs. Now that a fall nip was in the air, the sun felt delicious.

"Yes?" Ion asked, nodding in the direction of the decanter.

"How could I say no?" I answered. "I'd be a fool. This could not be more perfect. I'm so glad I let you take charge for a while. Bring me out here. It's hard for me to give up control most of the time. At home I'm known as a 'Type A,' a bit too fixated on having things just so, just the way I want them. Not a bitch, mind you. Just particular."

Ion raised his eyebrows, and forgetting my earlier self-imposed ban, I laughed heartily.

"You know, your laugh was the second thing I noticed about you. Or make that the third," he said, with a comical leer. "I think it's even more raucous now! You might consider trade-marking it, considering recent events."

He handed me a drink and walked me out to the garden, showed off his herbs and grapevines. Told me the Latin names of flowers and plants. Like many Romanians, he made his own wine.

For dinner Ion suggested a newly famous—"Like you!" he'd said—restaurant with a tasting menu and its own huge gardens. I thought I recognized the name. I rummaged through my capacious bag and found it, on the card Mr. Eminescu had given me: "The Stable," in English. Obviously meant to appeal to foreign visitors, and maybe also the new crop of young multilingual hipsters.

"Aha! It *is* the restaurant I thought it was. After my talk in Brașov, an older gentleman who had asked me a question about hunger came up to talk to me. He told me a similar story to yours. The Dictator's people had taken over his family's land, but his family wasn't fortunate enough to get it back. I guess it must take some legal wrangling, and maybe they just didn't have the means. And then there is the cost of renovation. Come to think of it, a woman I met is also here to try to reclaim property. I'm so happy for you, that you have your heritage back.

"It must be terribly frustrating to know that something so lovely and meaningful is yours," I said, "but some fascist, and then some ridiculous laws, are keeping you from claiming it. I keep envisioning myself going back to Long Beach and finding my own home taken over by a madman, and being unable to convince anyone that it is in fact mine. It's practically Kafkaesque. Or, like a *Twilight Zone* episode.... Anyway, I digress, and digress! This man's son is the head chef. Yes, let's go there. I'll bet he does something special for us when he knows who we are."

Ion called and easily got a reservation once he said his name. Then he added to the hostess that he was bringing a special guest. Her voice pitched upwards at hearing my name.

"Yes, sir! We'll have the best table for you!"

The restaurant was located on a sprawling farm. Not only did they grow their own vegetables, fruits and herbs, and make their own premium wines, but the proprietors grazed their own lambs and cattle and pigs, raised their own chickens for meat and eggs, raised goats for cheese. The animals were slaughtered on the property, then the meat aged and cured in house.

A complex of stables served as food storage and meat locker, and the restaurant itself was inside of a huge barn, which retained its beams and made reference to its rustic history in the form of large, framed black and white photographs.

Other than that, the restaurant bore little resemblance to a barn. It was chic and somehow felt cozy in spite of the soaring ceilings: an effect of the thoughtful lighting. Noise was kept down by several floating absorbing panels hung here and there. The bar, cleverly separated from the dining room by a "wall" of thick, hanging ropes, ran along one side and was buzzing with customers. The tables were polished chunks of reclaimed wood, and the chairs were thickly padded with cream-colored upholstery. At the far end of the room almost the entire wall was taken up with huge windows that allowed patrons to gaze out at the gardens, orchards, and grazing animals.

I nearly gasped at the effect.

"This is breathtaking! Look! You can actually see the elements of your dinner! Well, I am impressed. And I've been to many, many restaurants."

Ion squeezed my hand across the table, obviously happy he'd made this suggestion.

We'd been seated near the enormous window. On the table, fresh bread and butter and glasses of sparkling water were already laid out. Then one of the owners appeared with a bottle of fine effervescent wine, offered with his compliments. Fame does have its benefits.

Ion waved the owner to a seat, and he joined us in a glass so that I could chat with him for a little while.

The owner spoke a decent amount of English, but Ion stepped in to translate whenever communication seemed to be breaking down.

"I am awestruck by this place," I told him. "It is almost everything I would want a restaurant to be!"

The owner grinned, and told me the history of the place, the years it took to secure enough investors, the right sausage makers and cheese mongers and so on to get it opened and running the way the owners envisioned it. But the wait was worthwhile, because within weeks of opening it had become a "destination."

"And we have been operating at full capacity ever since!" he said.

At that I looked around and noted that, indeed, every table was either occupied or was being cleared for waiting diners. It made me smile, knowing that it was most likely Ion's name that somehow opened a table for us, and such a table, at such late notice.

I asked if at some point perhaps I could meet the chef, Mr. Eminescu.

"Of course!" the owner said. "He is a wonderful chef. You will see. We are fortunate to have him. Perhaps he can come out during your dessert. Things will be winding down a little by then."

We started our meal with the house charcuterie, served French style with *cornichons* and mustard.

"This is offal I can really enjoy!" I laughed.

"Can I lick your fingers for you?"

"Oh, no! I'm reserving that pleasure for myself!"

I dug into my delectable entrée—pork loin stuffed with fresh herbs, pears and caramelized onions, rubbed with a mustard sauce, and roasted till it was fork tender. At one point I stabbed a piece of meat with a delicious bit of crispy fat on it, and reached across to pop it into Ion's mouth. He moaned with pleasure.

"Food is so much like sex, don't you think?" I asked in a low voice, while running my foot up his ankle under the table.

"This reminds me of the eating scene in *Tom Jones*, only with less grunting." He was proud of his knowledge of things Anglo and American.

While we sipped our coffee and liqueur at the end of the feast, Ovidiu Eminescu appeared and bowed to us.

"Oh! Ovidiu! You don't mind if I use your first name, do you? I feel like I know you already, having met your charming father. Please join us. We've just been nearly struck dumb by your artistic cooking. I don't think I can breathe, I stuffed myself so full!"

Several times now I'd invited someone working in a restaurant to join me at a table since I'd been in Romania, and tried to remember when I'd last done any such thing in the States. Ah, being a stranger can be liberating. When one is not expected to know the protocol, one may break the little rules.

Ion stood and shook Ovidiu's hand warmly.

"Now that I know what a fine meal I can get here, I will be back. I have a country home near here. Sadly, I won't always have such a charming dinner companion," Ion said.

"This is a great honor sir," Ovidiu said. "You are a hero to me and to millions of us. My mother. My mother would be so proud that I am able to meet you."

As he took his seat he turned to me.

"Thank you so much for signing my book," he said. "I am a big fan of you. I regret that I missed your lecture." He stammered a bit, thinking I would mistake his meaning for the site of the murder. "The one in Brașov, I mean." He brightened. "I've ordered you a special dessert. It is my treat. That is correct? 'My treat'?"

At that I groaned comically and put my hands on my stomach.

"Do not worry," Ovidiu said. "I am having it wrapped for you to eat later, when you again are hungry."

"Oh, thank goodness!"

After what felt like a stolen night and day, we reluctantly drove back to Bucharest the following evening, where my tour was to resume the next morning. As we approached the city,

Ion grew quiet and my mood darkened. Ugly realities awaited.

PART IV

1

A bitter cold morning, and, still feeling dead tired, I climbed out of bed and stood in bare feet on the cold tiled bathroom floor, looking at myself in the mirror. The sinus congestion had returned.

I'd been having terrible nightmares. Ana, looking ghastly and wearing a crimson necklace, had come to me and asked me to look into what had happened to her. I'd said I didn't know what I could do. I was a foreigner, couldn't speak the language. I said, "I don't understand." But Ana had insisted that I was the only one who could help her.

And then, looking nearly like a phantom himself, Radu had appeared, and seemed to be pleading in some strange language for help. I couldn't understand him, and asked him to speak English, but he had continued in this alien language. I had then run across Ştefania, Matt, and Sophie, but all were mute.

I'd heard a hideous noise and run away, searching for a safe place.

Then I was in a dream version of the museum office with Magda and Mihai, Cozma artifacts strewn around the room. They'd said they were looking for something but didn't know what it was. Could I come back later, and we would talk then? I tried to find an exit, but there were only walls. The room went dark, and when the lights came on Dick Elbow stood in a room that resembled a jumble made up of his Consulate office and the Cozma Cabinet. When I asked him to help he merely turned away.

I'd seen Anca. Or, someone who was a combination of Anca and Ana. I somehow knew that Anca-Ana could tell me something, but Anca-Ana couldn't speak because the scar had moved from her hand and had become her *mouth*.

At some point in the dream I'd searched for Ion but couldn't find him. Finally, I'd tracked him down, way up high in the mountains, sitting by himself, and asked him what to do.

You wouldn't understand.

Though I felt as if I had not slept at all, I was glad to be out of bed after such a night. I showered quickly and stepped into a clean set of clothes, threw a few things into a suitcase, grabbed my laptop, and took the elevator downstairs. I felt lousy, but not sick enough to stay in bed.

I dreaded this tour, the energy I'd have to find to speak. I wasn't sure what I wanted, exactly. Being in Bucharest I would have to grapple with the crime, try to help. I felt I could contribute something, if nothing else comfort and commiseration to the kids who had lost a close friend to meaningless violence. Being in the country I would be lulled by Ion's company into forgetfulness. I had to resist calling him. I'd have to wait to see him till after the tour was over.

I wasn't sure what I'd say to Radu. Maybe nothing. Maybe just hug him. But maybe what he needed was to immerse himself in work, to feel he was taking care of me.

Yet Radu was nowhere to be seen. I searched the large lobby, peering behind pillars, scanning the many faces, and then briefly stuck my head out the front door, thinking he might be out there having a quick cigarette. I tried the café, but, except for a few men in business suits, no one was there except a stout, middle-aged woman in a brown coat, drinking tea.

I started to leave, but the woman stood up, saying, "Mrs. Unwin. I am Mrs. Năstase. I am sent by the Consulate. I am here to take you to Iași."

"I don't understand," I said. "Where's Radu."

"He is not able to come," the woman said. "He is occupied now." Her expression was deadpan. No smile, nothing. She looked rather sturdy.

Well, of course Radu would have to call off accompanying me on the tour. He must be feeling terribly depressed. I was sorry not to be able to comfort him. I hadn't seen him since Magda told him what had happened. I recalled a bit of my nightmare. Ana's body, and the scarlet necklace. The dream nagged at me.

"I'm thinking I should cancel the rest of my tour, after the terrible events. I feel as if it would be best for me to stay in Bucharest, helping my young friends. I don't think I'd be very engaging, now, anyway. I'm sure I would let people down. And I'm feeling a little under the weather."

The woman listened, watching me impassively.

"That is impossible," she said. "Arrangements have been made. We must go to the north. You are expected there, and many people look forward to meeting you and hearing about your writing." She grabbed my bag.

I couldn't find the energy to fight this block of a woman. And maybe a couple of days away, working, would help clear my head, so I could think clearly. Being with Ion certainly didn't have that effect. If anything, I felt foggier around him. Till then I wouldn't be any help anyway.

"We're going to miss our train if we don't hurry, aren't we?"

The woman said, "We are not taking the train, Mrs. Unwin. There has been a change of plans. We are riding to Iași in a car, provided by the US Consulate."

"A change of plans! Why? I thought the train tickets were already bought, and the itinerary set."

I looked down at this dowdy, officious woman. In her dreary coat and bundled hair, she seemed like a relic from the bad old days, and the prospect of being trapped with her on a long car trip was unappetizing. At least on a train you can get up and walk around.

"A car has become available, Mrs. Unwin. It is better than a train. More comfortable, and at one's disposal when needed. The train to Iaşi is not so good as the trains in Transylvania. It will be better to have a car."

"I'm not married, so it's *Ms.* Unwin," I said, "if any title is necessary. You can call me Vita, if you like." I tried to smile at the woman.

"Of course, my apologies," Mrs. Năstase said, and began walking toward the door with my bag.

A person can't help liking some people and not liking others. I decided long ago that there isn't much I can do about it. Occasionally I have changed my mind about people I initially disliked, but the truth is this seldom happens. My first impressions have generally transpired to be trustworthy.

2

The car turned out to be a minivan, with a driver who looked straight ahead, unsmiling for the several-hour ride. We passed through the urban wasteland of the city's perimeters and into the soggy pasturelands of the eastern side of the country. I didn't spend much time looking at the landscape. Mostly I dozed. And when awake, I tried to write notes about *Last Supper* on my laptop, attempting to recall exactly what it felt like to see the sculpture in actuality. I wasn't happy with the results. My sentences seemed desultory and banal.

Between naps, thoughts would come to me involuntarily, and I couldn't help feeling stuck on the details of the scene. The smashed glass, the bloody necklace.

Mrs. Năstase said little during the entire five and a half hour ride. She was occupied with a briefcase full of paperwork.

Iași converged on the grand white plaster and marble university district, with a walking mall running up from a substantial plaza to the semi-urban campus. It was a mix of concrete blocks and green strolling parks abutting the university quarter. The city seemed built for people who liked to stroll and sit in parks, hold convivial conversation, watch passersby. But I couldn't concentrate on the spectacle. I was distracted by my thoughts.

I noted a few of the gentle stray dogs, and wondered what became of them when the winter came.

They'd installed me in another sizeable hotel, this one named after a Roman emperor who had occupied Moldavia, the region Iași was capital of. No Romani women and children loitered outside of the hotel. Was it too cold here?

My mood changed when I met my host, who turned out to be the Romanian translator of my book. The man was an American Studies professor at the university, and introduced himself as Mihail Braunstein, and then said, "But please, Vita, call me Mike. It's my American name!" We both laughed.

"Oh, so you're the one responsible for all this! I'm glad to meet you. Romanians must like the translation. In Bucharest crowds of them jammed in to hear my talk. It was mind-boggling."

"I heard!" he said. "But I don't think it's the translation. Your book is absorbing. It was easy to work up the enthusiasm to write the translation." And we talked for a while. He'd enjoyed the book immensely, he said.

"Translators are asked by Romanian publishers to knock off lots of books these days," he said, "and most are just meat and potatoes, so a lot of them get rather indifferent translations. But

I had read yours while in the States, and really wanted to translate it. I pitched it to your publisher here, and the rest is history."

It was charming the way he used American colloquialisms. It made me trust him immediately.

"Well, I owe you a drink, then, Mike!" And off we marched to the hotel bar, the dour Mrs. Năstase in tow.

Drinking a glass of amber-colored white wine, Mike told me about his life, his spouse, Corina, and kids, his job at the university, his travels in the States. He was a native of Iaşi, and very proud of the city. "It's considered the Romanian 'Cultural Capital,'" he said. "I'm a Jew, as well, and Iaşi is also considered the Jewish capital of Romania. We have an old theater here, and we still have a community, in spite of the terrible history."

"I'm Jewish on my father's side," I said. "My father was an English Jew, grew up in the Manchester Strangeways Jewish quarter. Think of it, the ghetto was actually called 'Strangeways.' Because my mother was a gentile, I didn't grow up Jewish, and I'm not observant. But I always feel an affinity for the culture and of course the food."

"But your surname isn't Jewish," Mike said.

"The family was forced to change their name. It was a common occurrence for immigrants in early 20th-century England."

When Mrs. Năstase excused herself to find a restroom, I watched her walk away, then turned to Mike and said, "She was assigned to be my escort only today. I had a very nice young man named Radu, but he had to stay in Bucharest. I'm sure you would have liked him."

Mike glanced at the retreating Mrs. Năstase and smiled. "Your guide is rather ... mute, isn't she?"

"You could say that."

Feeling I could trust Mike, I wanted to tell him about Ana's murder. But before I could, Mrs. Năstase was suddenly there again, standing very close to me, saying, "Miss Unwin, we must now check in so that you will make it to the talk at the cultural museum in time." She took my arm to lead me to the check-in counter, but I brushed it off.

"I'm perfectly capable of walking by myself, thank you."

With its dim concentration-camp bulb in the solitary bedside lamp and the suicidal-yellow wallpaper, my room in the Roman ruler's hotel reminded me of past times. But the seedy room was a better fit for my increasingly foul mood than the up-to-date grand hotel room in Bucharest.

3

The museum where Harriet Beecher Stowe had talked looked just like a place where Harriet Beecher Stowe would have talked. Another ornate alabaster pile of rocks, with curlicues and cherubs hovering in the corners. I could picture her, the "little woman" reading from *Uncle Tom's Cabin,* "the book that started this great war."

I thought about war, and death, and bloodshed, and felt glum.

A guide briefly showed Mike and me, the ever-present Mrs. Năstase trailing, through the museum, and informed me that a reception would take place there but not the talk. It was not large enough to accommodate the kind of crowds I now attracted. I was taken to an auditorium at the university, which was filled beyond capacity.

Despite the large crowd, when I walked in the applause was rather feeble-sounding, and only a few called out that distressing impersonation of my laugh. It seemed that most looked intently at me, and even dispassionately. I turned to Mike.

"What's going on? They're staring at me as if I were a museum exhibit." My throat seized up.

Mike said, "I should have warned you, but I wasn't sure myself what would happen. I'm pretty sure that most of them are here because of the murder. They want to see you because it's become a sensational crime."

So Mike knew about the incident.

Mrs. Năstase stepped between us, saying, "I am ready to translate for you, Miss Unwin."

I glared at the woman, no longer even trying to hide my antipathy for her. "Mike is a brilliant translator," I said. "He translated my book, and it's a success here in Romania because of it. I'd like him to translate for me, if he's willing."

Mike said he would be glad to, but Mrs. Năstase would have none of it: "No, I am sent here to translate for you. I must do it. It is my job." She was resolute.

I decided to give an abridged version of the talk, and then get out of there. I certainly wouldn't be taking any Q&A.

"Everything old is new again," I started with little enthusiasm but with resolve, to do it and get it over with. Of course I'd have to skip the part I'd worked up with Radu about the multisyllabic food chemicals. But I cut other parts too, anything that was meant to seek common ground with the audience, or to give the audience a smile. I just didn't feel it, and so I went on....

"The food we ate used to be homemade, made from 'scratch,' we used to say. Bread made from wild yeast, unbleached flour and water. Beef from cows that graze local pastures, and are slaughtered locally. The farmer knew the cattle, and we knew the farmer.

"Now local farmers and restaurants work together to create a culinary experience. It seems a bit odd to pair 'restaurant' with 'farm,' as the farm was originally the place where one raised one's own food, and ate it at home. People were close to their food, as close as they could be. They knew it from ground up, what it ate, if animal, how it acted during a thunderstorm. If vegetable, they knew how far it turned toward the sun, how thirsty it was, how long it could be left underground before it began to rot.

"When I was a child, food mechanization and convenience were all the rage. Busy workers wanting to squeeze a few extra minutes out of a day by avoiding the arduous task of roasting or grilling or frying a cut of meat or piece of fish, washing and tossing raw ingredients for a salad, and baking a potato and slathering it with real butter. Real cooking need never be complicated or time-consuming, yet that is the idea fed to us. The result is as you see: heart disease, obesity, diabetes, environmental devastation, and so on.

"Let me say, I did not start my journey into food writing as an environmentalist. It is simply the way one has to be to write about food today. You have to understand the supply chain, and that the further one's food gets from its original manifestation, the lower its nutritional value, the greater the chance that it contains undesirable products, the more unknown the way it will affect the body, and the greater the number of resources it uses."

After briefly discussing my interest in offal, and how I came to it partly due to my previous experience in Romania, I brought my talk to a close and waited, exhausted, for the applause I expected to be polite rather than enthusiastic.

I hadn't anticipated quite such a level of disinterest, though. My talk was met with near silence, scattered applause coming from, I felt sure, the few actual fans of my writing. The rest of the crowd just gazed at me, mute.

At least some of the problem was with the translation. I'd noticed several times that when Mrs. Năstase translated something I'd said, audience members looked puzzled. I'd glanced over to Mike, who frowned.

What gets lost in the translation.

I could hear Radu reply, "The poetry, Vita, the poetry."

My head aching and my sinuses again filled with mucus, I glanced at the strange audience, smiled weakly, and exited before anyone could come up with a question.

At the reception, Mike introduced his spouse, Corina, who was warm and friendly. The others seemed to be skirting the topic they obviously wanted to hear about, intentionally showing that they would not bring it up, and I found this small talk more exasperating than the prospect of being directly interrogated about the homicide. Mike did his best to make me feel welcome, but I drank some wine and was uncommonly taciturn with the invited guests, people of the political ilk, academics, journalists, and NGO types. I was feeling a little drunk in less than an hour, and made an appeal for dinner. By then I was ravenous.

Mike and Corina took me to a restaurant that served traditional Moldovan cooking. Mrs. Năstase of course accompanied us, a shadow. I ordered the *ciorbă de vacuța* and *sarmale*, and felt much better after devouring the beef soup and stuffed cabbage leaves. However, this might have been actually due to the three shot-sized glasses of *țuică*, the filmy plum brandy I'd knocked back before dinner, a Romanian custom.

"How about some more of that ... plum brandy."

Mike and Corina exchanged glances, evidently a little concerned. Nevertheless, Romanians pride themselves on being genial hosts, above all. "No worries," Mike said. When I looked at him, he said, "I like to use Americanisms I've picked up whenever I can. You say, '*No worries*' for 'That's fine,' don't you?"

It made me grin. "Yes, many people say it."

Mike called the waiter over and ordered another round of plum brandies.

"Not for me," Mrs. Năstase said, waving her hand over the top of the full glass in front of her. She was an exceptionally tedious person.

"Don't be a killjoy. We're having an enjoyable Romanian dinner. We are talking about books and food and plum brandy. Have more!"

The waiter showed up and said something, and I said, "Wha'd he say?" I was holding my breath, trying to stifle the hiccups that wanted to come forth.

Mike laughed, saying, "He says they have a stronger *țuică*. It's called '*întoarsă*.' I'm going to thank him but say we want the ordinary stuff. It's strong enough, don't you think, Vita?"

"No, no! Bring on the whaddayacallit, the…'into-arse.' I'm a food *and* drink writer. I must try all kinds of libations if I'm going to stay informed."

"But it is so strong," Corina said, her English not quite as good as Mike's. "It gives the headaches." She tapped on her temple, and winked. She was smiling in a sisterly way.

Mrs. Năstase remained mute.

"I have some kind of sinus bug and sore throat, so could use the anesthetic." I turned to the waiter and said, "Bring on the into-arse!"

The man smiled and nodded, evidently comprehending, and soon came back with more of the translucent brandies. I took a swig of the drink.

"Holy—!"

I slammed the drained glass down onto the table, only just able to resist issuing a socially unacceptable oath. I was positive that this must be what lighter fluid tastes like!

A large extended family at another table laughed and nodded enthusiastically. It was a customary Romanian gag. Witnessing the vivid, comic reaction foreigners had to the national volatile compound.

4

Deposited back in the Roman emperor hotel, I watched the dreary room spin under the jaundiced light of the solitary lamp. I fell asleep, finally, and woke to the hotel room phone ringing at 9:30. It was Mike, who wanted to meet for breakfast. He could come by the hotel, and we could eat there or go somewhere close.

As soon as I put the receiver in its cradle, the phone rang again, its clamor not helping my hangover headache. This time it was Mrs. Năstase, reminding me that we must be on the road to Constanța before noon. I said I was meeting Mike for breakfast in an hour. The comment was met with silence. Then Mrs. Năstase said, "We do not have time for that, Miss Unwin. We must leave very soon."

"You said yourself we don't need to leave until late morning. We can depart at 11:30," I said and slammed down the phone. It incensed me, how this woman tried to control my every move, so I sat on the lumpy bed for a few minutes, waiting for the anger to subside.

Somehow, even though bending over to pull up jeans or put on socks made my head spin, I managed to get ready and go downstairs. Last night's libations had staved off thoughts of Ana's murder, but now they were back, nagging at me.

Mike was sitting in the hotel café, drinking a Turkish coffee, and Mrs. Năstase was next to him, looking characteristically stout and galling, drinking a tea.

Damn her. I had intentionally not invited her, but there she was.

A TV set hung on the wall, set on mute. It was a news program.

"The breakfast here is not bad, actually," Mike said. "And it's started to snow outside, so we may not want to bother going out for breakfast."

Masses of thick white clusters were drifting down into the streets, already starting to fill crevices and gutters. Living in southern California, I loved to see snow. It was lovely, but I agreed that there was no need to go out.

I ordered a plate of fried eggs and *brînză*, a sheep's milk cheese, along with bread, jam, and a slice of smoky ham. The only coffee was the Turkish variety, which would be fine as long as no sugar was dumped into it. And I wanted cream, as well. The waiter, a thin middle-aged man with a bald pate, seemed perplexed by this, but Mike reassured him that that was my real order, so he brought me a cup of the sludgy coffee and a small container of cream. It was a perfect hangover breakfast, and I dug in.

"I think I was a little out of control last night. Sorry if I made a scene, Mike." I'd been thinking about the little French professor in Cluj, and feeling embarrassed.

"Hooey!" Mike said. "You were in fine form."

Hooey. I smiled, thinking about the word, and, a reflex action, glanced at the TV.

I was stunned to see on the screen the image of Radu and Ana, side by side, two photographs placed next to each other, their names underneath the photos.

The picture of him made Radu looked shifty and dull-witted.

The photo of Ana was of … *her corpse.*

"Oh, my God, *what is that?*"

Mike turned in his chair to see, and looked back at me. His mouth was slightly open.

Mrs. Năstase was up, remonstrating with the waiter.

"Turn up the sound!" I said loudly. The waiter looked at me, as Mrs. Năstase seized his arm and pushed him toward the TV. "Yes, turn it up, for God's sake!"

"She wants him to turn it off!" Mike said. "*She's telling him to turn it off!*"

I rose and strode across the room to the waiter, who, alarmed, watched my tall frame draw near.

I roared at him, "TURN UP THE GODDAMN SOUND!"

Mike, behind me, was saying something loudly to the waiter in Romanian. Mrs. Năstase held one of the waiter's arms, trying to grab the other.

But with his other hand the fellow reached across the bar for the TV's remote and turned off the mute.

I stared at the image of Radu and Ana, completely mystified and feeling more and more uneasy. "What is it *saying?*"

"It's no concern of you," Mrs. Năstase said. "We must leave now!" She continued to talk loudly above the TV.

"*It's saying that the Gypsy murdered the Romanian woman,*" Mike said.

"It is for the police," Mrs. Năstase said, "and American visitors must not get involved. They have arrested the *Țigani* scum because he killed the Romanian woman."

I stood there like one of Cozma's sculptures, mute, uncomprehending.

"Radu is *Romani?*" I said, and, as I did, I realized that it was true—that I'd already known it. "And he has been accused of *murdering* Ana!" I knew in the core of myself that *this was not true.*

Mrs. Năstase said, "Miss Unwin, we must go to Constanţa *now*. You can *not* be late for your meetings there."

I looked at her as if she'd dropped from some alien planet. "I am going back to Bucharest immediately. *Now!*"

For the first time, Mrs. Năstase showed feeling. "You will *not* go to Bucharest until tomorrow when you will be *put on your plane* back to United States! You must come with me *now!*"

And she took hold of my wrists. I could feel the surprising force of the woman's strength, clutching me.

My body and brain in a fury, I drew up my full physical self and broke the woman's grip.

"*Do not touch me again!*"

I stepped closer, hovering over her.

Mrs. Năstase drew back. "I … will *not* take you to Bucharest. You can *not* use the car. It is for *going to Constanţa.*"

"I don't give *a shit* about the car! I'll take a train back. And I am going to miss my flight."

A thought seemed to pass across Mrs. Năstase's eyes, and she sneered. "I will not take you to the train station, and you will not get a taxi in this weather." She glared in triumph. "The taxi drivers refuse to work here when it snow."

"No worries," Mike said behind us. "My car is at your disposal." I turned to see him grinning at me.

Mrs. Năstase was beside herself. "You will regret that, if you do that!" she said to Mike. "*I warn you!*"

Mike looked at her. "I'm helping a friend," he said.

After kissing Mike on the cheek, I ran upstairs, grabbed my things, and ran downstairs. Mike drove to the train station.

On the way, I said, "I don't understand. It's so horrible and unbelievable. Radu couldn't have killed Ana. They were a happy young couple. They loved each other. And he never said that he is a Romani."

Mike said, "Some *pass*, as you say in English. European Jews have passed for centuries, even in supposedly enlightened countries like the UK and France. In this country, I can see how a Romani person would choose to conceal his identity."

I could see, as well, why Radu didn't confide in me. Too much lay in the balance. But now I knew that I must return to Bucharest and do what I could. And I'd get Ion to help. He'd know powerful people who would intervene on Radu's part. The dream came back, and I replayed the part with Ana's avowal that I was the only one who could help.

PART V

1

On the train ride back to Bucharest, I pondered every aspect of what had transpired. I understood now that Dick Elbow had tried to prevent me from becoming involved in the murder investigation, in a scandal. I wasn't sure whether he intended this for my protection or so that he wouldn't have to cope with problems that could arise as a result of my involvement, or a combination of both. I assumed no other reason could exist for his actions. In any case, I fumed over the thought of being prohibited from doing anything, and by my own government, and was ready to do what I could to help Radu.

I figured that the authorities conducting the investigation assumed Radu was culpable simply because he was a Romani man and Ana a Romanian woman. Even the TV news media portrayed him as a born criminal. So, I began in earnest to think over the murder scene in detail, trying to recall as clearly as possible what I'd seen in order to glimpse some possible design in the events.

I saw Ana's body on the floor, face up, vacant eyes open. I saw what seemed to be a choker necklace around her neck, her long chain necklace twisted so tight it cut into her skin. Her body lay in front of the display case of Cozma's documents. The glass top of the case shattered, the papers ransacked. I saw again the small, bulky-looking Cozma sculpture lying among the papers and glass. I recalled the glass fragments littering the floor, the light reflecting back in a grotesquely merry manner. And the glass shards glittering on Ana's ashen face. I saw *Last Supper*, impervious, in its bloody immensity.

Whoever had murdered Ana had done this because he or she wanted to break into the display case to search for something. Ana, entering the room to prepare for the reception, must have barged in on the perpetrator, and he or she had murdered her, then broke into the display case with the small, heavy Cozma statue and searched through the papers.

The murder happened first. The glass shards were on Ana's face—she had been choked before the killer had broken into the display case. *Garroted*, I thought grimly. And by her own necklace. Did the murderer find what he or she was looking for, and what could it be?

I retraced the contours of *Last Supper* for some sort of clue, concentrating on the figures rather than the food, returning to the central, most monstrous figure, the masked human-animal being that occupied the traditional Last Supper position of Christ—yet was not—his hand upturned, blood on the palm. The one that had sparked much conjecture.

There had to be some relationship traceable between Ana's murder and *Last Supper*. It was hardly the work of a freak or a psychopath. It appeared deliberate. And of course, the statue outed people who would object to being outed. It had just never occurred to me that any of the people represented would still be alive, alive and still living in Romania.

I brooded over this question for several hours, but by the time the train reached the Bucharest central station I'd arrived at no explanation.

Despite his wanting to keep me out of it, I sought Dick Elbow's help. I grabbed a taxi to the hotel and tried to call Ion. He didn't answer, so I left a message, letting him know what had happened, and imploring him for help. I said I was going to try to talk with Elbow right away, but could use his help, his connections.

The uniformed doorman summoned me a taxi. Standing there waiting in the cold, I looked at the small group of Romani women and children. Small people with small hands out, quietly appealing for a small donation. I thought about Radu, his faculty for the Romani language, and of course now understood. I gave each of the undersized, withered-looking women some money, and they bobbed their dark heads in thanks. I couldn't see Radu in these women and their children. But I realized that he had managed to deceive many people, not just me, an outsider.

At the Consulate, I passed through security, watched by the sturdy-looking Marine, with his uniform of white cap, tan shirt and tie, blue pants with red stripe. Another gatekeeper. Like the hotel doorman.

I made my way through the Embassy compound and walked into Elbow's office. His assistant's eyes widened at me.

Unsmiling and looking a bit anxious, the woman said, "Mr. Elbow is busy right now."

"You tell Dick Elbow that if he doesn't see me right now, I'm going to call my congressional representative. But I'm going to the Bucharest police first!"

Another Marine, as tall as me, appeared behind me, cradling a rifle. The woman must have silently summoned security. The mute Marine watched me intently, his weapon pointed at the ceiling, his finger on the trigger.

Elbow came out from his office, putting on his suit jacket. He waved the Marine away, and said, "Come with me, Ms. Unwin."

Inside, I refused to sit. "You sent that woman with me to make sure I didn't get back to Bucharest to help Radu!"

"I heard about it," Elbow said, sitting behind his desk, looking at his computer screen. "I'm sorry she behaved like that. We contract in-country residents to do jobs on occasion that we can't do, and sometimes they misunderstand our instructions and exceed our wishes." He looked at me. "You don't seem to be any the worse for wear."

"You have no right to prevent me from doing anything!"

"Actually, that isn't true," he said. "But I wanted to help you stay out of trouble. You could be detained in this country if you're caught up in a murder case. You don't want that, do you?"

"I *want*," I said, "my government to not interfere with me, and with doing what's right! I want to speak to the police. Radu is being accused of murder only because he is a Gypsy. I want to know what evidence they have that could make them arrest him. You are my representative in this country. I want you to help me."

He leaned forward, saying, "I've talked to the Ambassador, Ms. Unwin. Here's the situation. If you stay any longer beyond your planned visit, and get involved in this murder investigation, you will be on your own. Your hotel reservation will be canceled, and you will have to pay for your own flight home. You will no longer have any special arrangement with the Embassy and Consulate. You will be treated like any ordinary US citizen."

"Just don't interfere with me again, or I will call my representative," I said over my shoulder as I walked out.

In the car, I tried calling Ion again, but this time didn't bother leaving a message when he didn't pick up.

2

When I got back to the hotel, I discovered that my room

reservation had already been canceled. They certainly kept their word. I requested another room, and asked to' have my things moved there. This would take some time as the hotel was booked up, the clerk said. Finally, I was put in a smaller room— my things brought in. The room was in the back of the hotel, without a view of the square. I didn't care. I'd seen enough of the country.

I sat in the one armchair and tried to call Ion again. This time he answered.

"I hope you're all right!" Ion said. "This is all so incredible, like the bad old days. I don't understand how Elbow could have done such a thing. Of course, I will do everything to help, but I'm afraid I'm not available today. I can have my driver pick you up and take you to the police. Sit tight. He will call on you at the hotel. After you have talked to the police, I will come by tomorrow evening and take you to my house in Sinaia, and we will sort this out. I'm sure we'll find a solution."

This was disappointing. I'd hoped he'd come right away. But of course he'd have important obligations that he just couldn't get out of. We talked for a few more minutes, Ion cooing that everything would fine. When I hung up, I lay on the bed for a while, half dozing, and feeling both fatigued and agitated.

I woke to the room phone ringing, the desk saying that a driver was waiting. I went downstairs and saw the man, who nodded. He evidently didn't speak English.

He took me to the police station, which wasn't far away, and parked the car, indicating that he would wait for me there. I walked into the concrete block building and asked if anyone spoke English. The reception officer shook his head, got up, and came back with a young, gorgeous policewoman. One of those stunning Romanian women with auburn hair and large, hooded eyes. I was slightly startled at the sight of her. Her radiance seemed disturbingly incongruous in the circumstances.

"Yes, what you want?" the young woman said.

"I'm here about the murder of Ana ..." I realized I didn't know Ana's last name. "The girl who was killed at the National Gallery, in the Cozma Cabinet."

The policewoman gazed at me with those dark glittery eyes. "You are American writer, no?" she said.

"Yes, Vita Unwin. I am a US citizen, and I witnessed the scene of the murder only moments after it took place. I have some important information about the crime that I'm certain the investigators could use."

"We have the man that did it," she said. "Tell me why do you want to speak to someone here."

I didn't see the good of explaining the situation out here in the corridor, but tried to be understood: "I know that the man you have couldn't have done it. He was in a relationship with the victim. He loved her. He wouldn't have killed her. Just the opposite. May I now talk to the investigators for this case?"

The policewoman studied me for a moment, and said, "The *Țigani* confessed the crime. The case closed."

I stared at this Romanian beauty in cop drag, trying to digest her baffling statement. "What do you mean, he's 'confessed'! He wouldn't do that unless ..." I considered for a moment. *Unless he was coerced.*

"I want to talk to the investigators right now!"

"You have no role in this. You are not Romanian." The glamorous young woman turned on her heels and walked with faultless poise back down the tiled hall, an unreal runway model in cop costume.

3

I stood in the doorway of the museum office. Inside, Magda and Mihai on hands and knees sorted through papers that were strewn around the room. The room was in violent disarray, as if an angry someone had wanted to smash things but could only find items to tear and throw.

"What happened here? It wasn't like this, was it?"

Magda, looking weary and tear-stained, snapped, "Of course not! Someone tore it apart, dumped boxes out. Even cut open some and damaged the papers. So much work, gone!"

"Not gone," Mihai said, softly. "It's all still here, as far as we know. And we know what goes in what box, at least the boxes that were done. We have the catalog notes. It's just a big mess that we need to clean up and sort out. It's not that bad."

"Okay, I'm really tired. I'm sorry, Vita. And I'm mad. We all know Radu didn't do it," Magda said. "The idea is absurd, idiotic, ridiculous, and racist. 'Of course he did because he's a *Țigani.*' Right."

Magda sat on her heels with her arms tightly crossed across her chest, and I could see that she was clenching her teeth by the slight movement of her jaw.

"The police won't talk to us," Mihai said. "They questioned us, but they didn't listen to what we said. They just asked us questions and talked at us. We can't see Radu, either. How can we help him? I feel like I've lost two of my best friends now."

Magda nodded.

"Me, too. At least I still have you, Mihai," she smiled weakly. "Nothing better happen to you."

"You have to help us, Vita. We're going crazy here. You're an outsider. You know people," Mihai said. "All we could think of to do was to put some posters around with a picture of us and Radu at the bar, just to show that he's our friend, and saying we know him and he didn't do it. And can anyone help us. The police don't care. We called about this break-in, and when they came they threw us out while they looked around. But they didn't act like they thought it was very important."

"I'm not getting any help from the Consulate, that's for sure," I told them. "Ion is seeing what if anything he can do. But I feel helpless, too. And I hate feeling helpless. Why don't we try. Try to at least sort out what we know and don't know. Doing something is better than doing nothing."

We started charting the facts as we knew them.

"It all happened inside the Cozma Cabinet," I said. "Ana was killed there, or at least there's no reason to think she wasn't."

Madga drew a square on a sheet of paper, and named it Cozma Cabinet.

"She lay in front of the case of documents. Put that there."

Magda drew a rectangle and a stick figure.

"*Last Supper* was about there."

Madga drew.

"Before my talk, Ana was alive. We all saw her. When the lights went down, I couldn't see anyone. Was the Cabinet locked? No, of course not, Ana was still setting up the reception and probably keeping an eye on things.

"Okay. The case was broken. Ana's body and face were covered with glass, so she was lying there when the case was broken. Did you figure out if anything was missing?"

"That is a problem," Magda said. "The Cabinet is taped off and guarded and no one will let us in to look. Ana chose the documents and laid them out herself. But she took notes, she always did—she was very methodical about her work. Her notes should be somewhere in this chaos."

Magda almost looked like she was going to cry as she

surveyed the mess that represented so much work, work she'd cheerfully given extra time to in order to be with her friend, to be doing something important.

"I don't know if we'll continue," she said. "It seems ruined now."

"I know from my own setbacks and bad times, just do one thing now. One thing at a time. That's the way to get through," I said, giving Magda's shoulders a little squeeze.

"So, someone ransacked this room, looking for something. We don't know what, or if he or she found it. But maybe we can figure it out," I said.

We agreed that we should find the exhibit notes before anything else, which would mean sorting through the mess of papers. Mihai volunteered to run out for pizza and beer. Magda and I got to work. It would be a long night.

When a weak fall light came through the little window the next morning, the office was considerably neater, two pizza boxes and six cans of beer neatly set by the door, twenty-some piles of papers of various kinds arranged either in boxes or on or under a long table. One pile held letters to or from family members, another letters to or from artist friends, another other friends. One pile held juvenilia, such as early sketches and school essays, another personal photographs. There were separate piles for documents dealing with specific artworks. We'd placed damaged documents in one box to deal with later. In one larger box we'd laid everything we hadn't decided how to categorize yet.

Another box contained everything we'd found that mentioned or in any way dealt with *Last Supper*, regardless of the type of document: letter, sketch, notes, whatever. In a neat faux-leather-bound folder, we found Ana's notes for the exhibit.

She'd drawn the room layout, light positions, case and stand

Volume 17

positions, positions of wall art, outlined the large space for *Last Supper*, identified everything to go in the cases and wall displays.

In my memory I recreated the room before and after the murder to try to see what was missing. I set in place all of the individual art pieces, each sculpture, drawing and painting. I saw the smashed case and the glass and the small sculpture. Next to the small sculpture and among the shards was an empty space. The case had held fifteen pieces. I counted from the left, one, two, three, the fourth a stub like a ticket stub set above a travel visa, the fifth some sort of letter, then where the sculpture lay in the glass, the sixth, the sixth piece, that was either moved or missing.

We checked Ana's notes with my memory. The sixth item over was a sketch of *Last Supper*, as Ana described it, a quick sketch Cozma must have done just to get the layout right, place the table and the figures and the food, almost an outline, with vague features on the faces. It must have been an early workup of the piece, with the details to be filled in later.

I played through my mind the Cabinet, the notes, the glass, the missing sketch.

4

The message this time was from Anca. "I want to talk to you. I must. It's important. And it will help your young friend."

Curious and hopeful, I agreed to meet her in a café near the hotel, the one in which I'd taken refuge from the pursuing street mob—what seemed like so long ago now.

"I wondered what'd happened to you after the talk," I said as I sat down. "I looked around for you and you were gone."

"I saw in the newspaper that you would be speaking at the

National Gallery about *Last Supper*," Anca said. "I already wanted to see it, and I was going to tell you and the students what I knew about him, Cozma—Anton—that I knew him well. We were friends in Paris. Romanian creative people are bound to find each other in Paris. But when I walked up behind you, I saw the dead girl, and then I heard *his* voice. I heard it and I disappeared. I'd hoped never to hear that voice again. I cannot imagine how you must feel knowing who you have been in love with."

"What are you talking about? Who?"

"*Ion Vadim*. He did *this* to me."

Anca laid her hand on the table for me to get a good, close look.

Looking openly at the scar now, I instinctively recoiled. Like a stigmata, I thought. "You're crazy. That is the most ridiculous thing I've ever heard. Ion could never harm anyone. He was a writer, exposing the crimes of the regime. He's a national hero!"

"Look," Anca said. "I know this is hard, but you must believe that he is a fake. He is a dangerous man."

"How can you even say this to me? You are a liar or crazy. I don't understand why you'd want to say these things."

"I am sorry. You are wrong. I am not mistaken. He is not who he says. He lied to the whole country, but I know the truth."

I rose abruptly, and with as much self-control as I could manage, threw a couple of bills on the table and stormed out, followed by several sets of curious eyes.

As I walked out, I could hear Anca behind me, saying, "Wait, Vita,…"

In the street, I stopped, thought for a moment, and then, though I'm not sure why, turned to go back.

But Anca had disappeared.

5

When I got back to my room I immediately called Ion. In about fifteen minutes, he was in front of the hotel in his expensive, shiny new French car, and we started for his house in Sinaia. It was now dark and cold out, and warm inside of Ion's car.

In spite of this warmth, after the business with Anca I was feeling especially anxious. "Have you had any luck with the police?" I asked.

"Unfortunately, no. You see, I am not as important as you think I am," he said. "And, I'm sorry to say this, but I'm afraid it is very possible that he did it, Vita. The police say he has confessed."

"So they told me. But it's bullshit."

Ion was silent for a moment.

"Are you all right?" he asked.

"Yes, I'm sorry," I said in lower tones. "I just had a very unnerving encounter with a woman I barely know. She said ... she said ... Oh, hell. It's not even worth saying. She is obviously crazy."

Ion said nothing for a moment, evidently thinking. "I wonder if this is the same one. The police told me something else, about a woman named Anca. It seems that she broke into Ana's office on the night of the murder. Her fingerprints were all over the place."

I paused a moment to take in this remarkable information. "Anca? That's her name. Why would she do that?"

"They don't know, Vita. But they assume she's linked to the murder. They were looking for her in Cluj." He paused. "But evidently she's here in Bucharest."

"Then they must release Radu immediately! If they think

she's the one who did this, it's obvious that Radu is innocent, just as I've been saying!"

Ion listened. "They say they found Radu's prints all over the office, too, so are not ruling out a conspiracy involving the both of them. My sense is that they think Radu and this Anca were working in cahoots."

I almost laughed at the expression. *In cahoots.* Like the dialog in some old film noir. It somehow fit the swift, smooth drive across the nocturnal landscape, the bright headlights in my eyes.

"Of course Radu's fingerprints would be all over the office. Ana was his girlfriend, for Christ's sake, and he's been working with her on the Cozma project. Anyway, why would they conspire to kill Ana? They don't even know each other!"

"How do you know this?" Ion said, coolly. "Do you know this for sure?"

I had to admit to myself that I didn't. I wasn't happy with Ion's response. I wanted support right now, not this questioning.

"But why did this fugitive come to me, then," I said, "and say to me that you're not who you appear to be, that you are a 'dangerous man'?"

Ion kind of laughed. "She said *what?*"

"Yes. That's the crazy business I was talking about a few minutes ago. I know it's insane, but why did she find *me* to say this to? And why would she risk exposure?"

He laughed softly again and said, "Yes, she's out of her mind. She saw me after the murder, recognized me from the old days. Mistook me for someone else."

I didn't say anything. I was thinking about it. We were both silent for a while.

Evidently, while he'd pondered the news, Ion's view on this had changed. He was no longer laughing. "Listen, Vita," Ion whispered. "This women is dangerous, going around saying things like this about me. There are people here in Romania who still remember the work I did as a journalist, people I made enemies of and who have hung on to their influence and high position. And these people would be very happy to see me trashed by the tabloids, my reputation dragged through the dreck. Vita, we must find this Anca and convince her that she's just confusing me with someone else."

"I understand that this is upsetting. But she just showed up, and when I told her she was mistaken, she vanished."

"You have no idea where she might have gone, what she might do?"

"Maybe she did go back to Cluj, and the police will find her soon. And they will establish that she killed Ana, and then release Radu."

"My only hope is to find this mad woman and talk to her before the police find her. She could ruin my reputation, everything I've achieved. When she meets me, and I tell her who I really am, she must see that I'm not who she thinks I am."

"Then, the only thing I can think of is that she will find me again. She found me once, and she can find me again. When I left her, she seemed to have something more to say to me. I assume she will want to tell me the rest."

"Yes," Ion said, "that does make sense."

Now the both of us were distressed. I tried not to look into the glaring yellow eyes of oncoming cars.

"My head is spinning," I said. "I'm angry like I've never been before and it's clouding my mind. And I'm getting sick again."

Ion didn't speak for a moment. "But shouldn't you go back to the hotel? How will she find you if you leave the hotel?" He seemed to be slowing the car down.

I was amazed. "I don't really want to be found right now!" I said. "I feel like I've had enough of this entire horrible affair for now. I can come back to Bucharest tomorrow afternoon, after I've gotten my head clear, and wait for Anca then. Though, I suppose the police might have the same idea."

I could hear Ion's breathing. "I hadn't thought of that. That is true," he said. "Of course, Vita." And he sped up again.

We were quiet in the car. I rested my hand on Ion's shoulder while he drove, and tried to feel the way I had before, the world going away, my head clearing, my mood brightening. But it wasn't quite the same.

In the silence, Ion slid a disc into the player. I recognized it. Mahler, "I Have Lost Track of the World."

6

Ion was in an uncharacteristically silent mood as he unlocked the front door of his house. He walked into the dim room, and in a moment an end table lamp was on. The room was still rather gloomy with the single light on. He fell into his deep leather chair.

I really needed a glass of something soothing on this cold, grim night. I rummaged around in the kitchen and found the makings of a simple meal: *saucisson sec, mămăligă*, and, in Ion's stainless wine fridge, a bottle of Saturnalia, the same Romanian red wine I'd had at the hotel restaurant when I'd first arrived and also at the restaurant in Cluj.

I sliced several pieces of the sausage and heated up the polenta on the stove, and then placed the food onto two small plates. I picked out two tall, stemmed, large-bowled Burgundy glasses, and found a sommelier knife and a tray, plucked the cork out of the bottle with the hinged corkscrew and poured the claret-colored wine about halfway up the glasses, then went back to the living room with everything on the tray: plates of food, glasses of wine, and bottle. I brought the corkscrew, as well. I knew we'd be opening another bottle. It had been that kind of day. Week.

It had calmed me to carry out these simple, commonplace activities.

We finished the bottle in silence.

Ion hadn't budged from the chair. He'd taken the food and wine and eaten and drunk, quietly. When done, he picked up the sommelier knife and began fiddling with it, pulling out the small trimming blade and repeatedly pressing it back into position, evidently lost in thought.

"We need another bottle," Ion said. "Let me show you my cellar. It's one of my favorite rooms."

We descended a long, narrow staircase with two turns in it. Ion had flipped a light switch at the top, but the space below was still dimly lit. I held the banister and paid attention to my footing.

At the bottom, the staircase opened onto a wide hall with a stone floor. Severe-looking black sconces cast a minimal amount of light on stone walls. The air felt damper and chill. Probably a perfect place for a wine cellar, but not for spending time on a dreary evening.

The hallway curved slightly, the end of the hall disappeared in darkness.

I laughed quietly, and said, "It's like a Vincent Price movie. Or a scene from *The Cabinet of Dr. Caligari*." I waited for him to laugh, too.

Ion reached behind a sconce and pulled out a key on a chain. He unlatched a heavy door and pushed it open. A flipped switch and soft lights came up, illuminating an extensive, impressive wine cellar. A tasting station was set up near the door, a round, tall wood table and curved-back chairs. Glasses and wine tools hung on a wall over a sturdy shelf. I could smell the loam of the vineyards.

The racks of wine seemed to go on forever, an effect of the lighting in the room.

"Some of the wine here is my own," Ion said, gesturing to some of the racks, "bottled from the vines on the property. Some bottles are older, awaiting their ideal opening year. Still others I've added over the past few years, both to age and to drink. I've become a collector. Of these and some other things."

Ion's voice had taken on a dreamy quality I hadn't heard before.

"I think this is a special occasion. We should open something to celebrate it," he said, pulling a 1989 Château Haut Brion off of a high shelf. "You'll like this wine. It's subtle, as French wines often are. It has a past, a story to tell us. We can taste the *terroir*. It has secrets, I am certain. A 1989, the year of the Revolution. Or, Coup, depending on how you look at it."

I watched him. With the sommelier knife, he pulled out the cork with a faint pop, poured the wine into two glasses, the sound of liquid splashing on the sides. The sucking sound as the bottle released its contents, every sound intensified in the stillness.

I took the glass.

"To undying love," Ion said, clinking lightly against my glass. "To a future of unparalleled beauty. To desires fulfilled.

"It's hard to believe that I once had to drink cheap dreck," he said. "*Dreck* is a good word, isn't it? It means 'filth,' 'trash,' even 'excrement. You see, when I went to prison I had to live on dreck. I ate garbage because I had to. I said to myself that I am going to endure, and when I survive this thing I will never eat anything but the best and never drink anything but the best."

I hesitated to speak, as the moment seemed fragile, somehow. My heart was doing little skips inside my chest, and I hoped he couldn't see. That I was apprehensive.

"Ion? It's a little ... cold down here."

"We will go back up in a while. We're not done yet. You've barely touched your wine, this exquisite wine I opened just to share with you. And I have something else to show you."

He pulled on one of the wine racks and it swung open.

"My secret room."

"I'm really tired. Maybe tomorrow, when this headache is gone."

Ion put an arm around me and began to move me into the room. I wanted to resist but felt compelled to see. *The truth.* He ushered me through the secret door, and I let him.

The room was square, plain. Plain stone walls. Plain stone floor. The only light came from a glaring spot lamp trained on a plain wooden table and a plain straight-backed chair.

"What is this?" I sized up the spare, unpleasant, ugly space.

He sort of laughed. "So much is forgotten after a big social and political change. People want to put the past behind them, and get on with life. They want to erase the past because they played a role in it, whether victim or persecutor—sometimes both. I wanted to retain some of that history to keep reminding myself of what happened.

"This is the way it looked. The room they used to break me down in. The glaring light. The stiff chair. Do you know that just being forced to sit straight in one chair for days at a time is a kind of torture? And how do you think it would feel to be in a room with a bright light constantly on?" He asked these questions as lightly as if he was asking me whether I would like another glass of wine.

"You were tortured. I know that." I considered his body in my memory. "But you have no physical scars."

"No, my marks are not visible. And I have managed to hide them with a cheerful outer surface."

I spoke slowly. "You need help, Ion. I can imagine that you still carry the pain."

"Well, Vita, honestly, you can't imagine. You can only … what? *Know*. You can know something, but you can't imagine it."

"I wouldn't understand, then."

"No, you wouldn't understand," he said, looking at me, and closing the door. He stood in front of the door, still staring at me, his eyes cold and empty.

A jumble of fear, horror, loathing, and sorrow washed over me. I could hardly believe what I was about to say.

"But I think I'm beginning to understand. What Anca said. Was there any truth in what Anca told me?"

"You want to hear something funny? You know that marvelous restaurant we went to, the one nearby that you so wanted to visit because you'd met the father of the amazing chef? And the chef," his laugh hollow, "*thanked me* for all I've done for the victims. Do you remember?"

I didn't answer.

"It's funny, because I was the one who put that man's father away for so many years. He was sent to prison for growing carrots. Can you imagine? The Dictator said that no one should grow any food that would feed just himself. Not even a few carrots. And this while people were starving, because the government was confiscating everything. People were starving while the Dictator and his family lived liked gods. So, you could go to prison for growing food that you fed your starving family!

"How did we find out those things? People *ratting on* one another to make points with the goons, hoping for a few miserable privileges. That's the expression, isn't it? 'Ratting on?'"

I said nothing.

"Of course, the Dictator's goons were ready to turn on everyone, even those who ratted on their neighbors. It was like an elaborate game.

"But think of it. This young man *thanked* me for being a national hero, and I'm the one who sent his father to prison for growing carrots to feed his starving son. You see, a game."

"What are you going to do?"

"The question right now," Ion said, "is what to do about you."

7

All the time he was talking, I stood still but scanned the room for something to help me, some instrument I could use to get out of this. On one wall was a small, carefully arranged collection of ugly devices, things that appeared made to hurt people. To pinch off skin, to break bones. And among them a couple of glittering knives, oddly shaped, but surely able to do the trick.

Now, could a person who's never physically harmed a soul manage to cut her insane lover up in order to escape her own death, or worse? That was the bizarre question flashing through my mind.

Tiredness gone, headache gone, sinus congestion gone, adrenaline pumping, I realized that I had a strong survival instinct. I'd find a way out.

From the wall display I plucked a glinting serrated dagger.

He looked at me, actually sad. "No, Vita, there's no need for that."

"Stand back," I said. "Stay back." I raised the dagger. I felt the heft of the thing, strangely well balanced and natural in my hand.

"I'm not going to hurt you, Vita. I could never hurt you. I want to get you out of Romania so that you are free from all of this, and can go back to your safe, beautiful life … on the beach." He smiled, as if picturing me on a beach. "In the goodness of time, I'll come to you again, in California, and we'll start over. You will learn to forget, just like everyone else has." His voice had a kind of void I'd never heard before.

"I couldn't do that," I said, watching him.

"Why not? Tens of thousands of people in this country and millions upon millions throughout time have done it. People who have done unspeakable things to other people. And then later they just go on, with their spouses and children, their jobs and homes, their bank accounts and their secrets. Their place in society. Just like in your country."

I said nothing, again.

"Yes, what your country has done to the black people, to the Indians, to many others, just like the way the Gypsies have had it here. And your country has done terrible things to people in other countries.

"What else can those who have benefited from others' losses do?" he continued. "Give themselves up and go to prison? Become saints? Give back everything they have? What's the point? What good would it do?"

I stared at him. Ion had disappeared. Or, rather, his mask had fallen away.

"So you're just like one of the figures in *Last Supper*?" I said.

"Yes, Vita, I am," he said, smiling.

He tilted his head down and began to approach me. A bitter spasm coursed down my spinal column. "No further," I said.

"Give me the knife, Vita," this stranger said, his eyes fixed on mine. "Hand me the knife."

"No!" I said.

"You think it's simple to stab someone with a knife? It isn't. It's hard, believe me. Have you ever stuck a knife into a living human body? You need to be strong, and fast, and find the right spot to stick it in. And you need to be someone who can hurt people. That, above all. What you really need is something that stops a person dead. You need a gun."

I repeated that he should stay away.

He said nothing, just approached me, unhurried, one hand out.

As I felt myself being backed against a wall, I suddenly and almost instinctively stepped toward him and scored the extended hand.

He screamed something foul in Romanian. Red beads appeared on his hand. He shouted the same epithet again.

But the wound was shallow. I could see that I had only grazed his hand, a diagonal band across the top veins. There would be no scar.

Ion seized me by both of my wrists, his face a crimson rage, his eyes inhuman. The dagger dropped to the stone floor, a dull thud.

Mutely, he kicked the door open and dragged me out of the room and up the stairs while I screamed to let go, let go, let go. I could feel the crushing strength in his grip on my wrists. Flailing, trying to free myself, I was banged against walls on the way up the stairs. He yanked and tugged and jerked and wrenched me up and on, relentlessly, unspeaking.

At the top of the stairs, he flung me into his study. I fell on the floor. He opened his desk drawer and began to fumble around. He was speaking Romanian, muttering oaths to himself.

8

"Are you looking for this?"

Anca held a pistol, pointed at Ion's heart. Her other hand was down at her side, holding a black notebook.

"Remember?" She then lifted the other hand with the notebook, with its deep, jagged scar, and held it up for Ion to see. I could see a white "17" printed on the notebook.

Anca spoke to me. "I found this wonderful thing in his desk. It's loaded."

He stepped away from the desk. "You broke into my house." He held his hand out. "Give me my gun."

"*His* house," Anca said, still talking to me. "Do you hear him? This is *my* house. He stole it from me. I didn't need to break in. I still have the key. He never had the locks changed. But why should he?

"I heard you two downstairs," Anca went on. "I was in there when you came in. I was hiding behind an old secret place, listening. You see, I know this house like no one else. No one else living, that is. This is my family home.

"Let me tell you something, Vita. That room is not a wine cellar. It's a crypt, a family crypt. Generations of my ancestors were interred there, and he evidently had them removed. I followed you and him up the stairs, softly. I would have shot him, but you were in the way."

Ion stared at her. "I had thought you were dead," he said.

She looked at him, but spoke to me. "Almost died, Vita. But my husband bought my freedom for me. It was his last act of love. One of *his* goons took the money and arranged to get me and our little daughter out of the country. You see, Vita, the entire system was corrupt. It was possible to deal if you had the money.

"My husband stayed behind in that foul prison, with no air, no sunlight, filthy water to drink, barely any food. Many starved. I hope my husband died a quicker, easier death. I know my husband told them nothing because he knew nothing to tell. He was murdered just as if he'd been shot in the head. He was a musician. He was a gentle person with no wish to harm anyone. Vadim took my love and my child's father. He kept my husband in that foul, stinking, airless hole until he died."

I still lay on the floor stunned. A little unstable, I got up.

"And he killed your friend, the young woman in the museum."

I looked at Ion. I knew it was true. I'd seen it downstairs.

"You have no heart. You won't feel a thing," Anca said as she lifted her arm and aimed the gun.

"Anca, no!" I said. "You don't want to kill him. You haven't killed anyone. What will they do to you if you do this?"

I grabbed Anca's hand just as she pulled the trigger, and with a deafening discharge a bullet rammed into Ion's thigh. He fell to the floor, reaching for and toppling a side table with a loud crash. Blood gushed from the wound.

My ears were ringing. I couldn't hear anything for a moment.

Anca stood statue-like, holding the gun. I gently pried her fingers from it. "Go to his bedroom, upstairs on the right," I told her, "and get a belt and my stockings. They're on a chair." She went up the stairs.

I could see that Ion was weakening. He was looking pale and

his eyes were having trouble staying open. The blood still flowed onto the carpet.

Anca returned with the belt and stockings.

I propped Ion up, got his hands behind his back and wound a stocking around and around his wrists, crisscrossing and winding so that they were securely tied. I looped the belt between his wrists, and buckled it around the leg of a solid-looking library bookcase. I then fished in the pocket of the jacket he'd slung across the back of the chair for keys and phone. I also put the pistol in my bag and backed out of the room, pushing Anca along behind me.

"I can't. I don't. I … I," I was stammering, almost overcome. "We have to go. We have to get out of here."

With Anca in the passenger seat, I revved up the car. I took off with a squeal that startled me. Slowed down.

"Keep your head, lady," I told myself.

The adrenaline pumping was probably the only thing keeping me from breaking down, I thought as we drove along mountain roads. Anca sat beside me, blank-faced.

I pictured Ion sitting in the growing pool of blood, so I pulled off the road.

"I think you saved my life," I said. "He had a look in his eye that I've never seen on anyone before. He was getting ready to hurt me, I know it. I believe you now. About everything. I do.

"But, Anca, you must make a call. He could bleed to death, and then you really would be a murderer. We have to make sure someone gets there before that happens. Try to find someone on his phone to call for help. Then, it can't be traced to us."

She looked at me and picked up the phone. She scrolled through Ion's phone numbers looking for nothing in particular, just a name. But it was another Vadim she ended up calling. Anca set the phone to speaker so that I could listen.

"*Tată?*" the confused voice asked. "Father?"

Anca told Vadim's son that his father had been shot. She told him his father was at his country house, with a serious wound. Anca ended the call.

I took her to the airport. We bought two strong coffees and sat in molded plastic seats. Anca held the notebook, sipping her coffee.

"I'm not leaving, Vita. I'm staying in Romania."

"What? They'll put you in prison for attempted murder. You have to leave."

"I can't run away. Vadim knows who shot him, and will tell the police. I would be arrested in France and sent back to Romania."

"It's worth a try," I said. "You could hide. You must know other Romanian people there who can help."

Anca sipped her coffee. "Anyway, I'm not staying because of that. I told you once that I wasn't sure whether I wanted to return to this country, that I wasn't sure if I wanted to be a Romanian again. But I *am* a Romanian, and I must stay here and face whatever I have to face. I heard what Vadim said to you in the crypt, about forgetting the past, just going on with one's life. He was right, if for all the wrong reasons, but I can't do that anymore. I must stay in Romania and become a Romanian again."

9

"How did you know, Anca?"

"In the Cozma Cabinet," Anca said, "I heard his voice and saw the violence and put them together. I knew what he was capable of, but I didn't know why he'd kill that girl. I had to think, so I disappeared. I know what people think of him, how revered and important he is. I knew I'd have to have it all figured out.

"There had to be a connection to the exhibit. Cozma had told me that he'd made a key of the figures in *Last Supper*, but hadn't told me who they represented. He was afraid of putting me and others in danger with that knowledge, so that is all he told me.

"That is what Vadim was looking for when he smashed the case, *the key*, but he didn't know what it looked like. Your young friend must have interrupted him when he was searching the papers," she said, "and he murdered her right there.

"I knew when I saw that girl and the smashed glass and heard his voice that he was her killer. He'd been in charge of 'disciplining' political prisoners, but we were all 'political prisoners' in those days. He never actually dirtied his hands, but he gave the orders. He lied to the whole country, but I knew the truth. You do not forget the voice of the one who did this to you, and who hurt people you loved. You don't. Ever.

"During the chaos after the murder I ransacked the curator's office looking for something among Cozma's things that would reveal Vadim's guilt. I knew I had to get to it before he did. And I found it. It's called Volume 17."

"This," I said, indicating the black notebook.

Anca nodded.

"This drawing shows who is represented by each figure," she said, turning to a page that fell open easily. "He was the one in the middle. The blood on his hand was my blood. Mine and others."

I stared at the drawing. It was the Ion I'd first met, even younger. He sat at the table, in the center, mouth open with raucous laughter, hand raised as if he'd just told a hilarious joke.

But it wasn't the Ion I'd met. It was the Ion I'd seen that night.

The table was strewn with glasses and the remains of a feast.

The Dictator sat to the left, indeed in the spot traditionally occupied by Judas.

Each figure was numbered and keyed to a page, which described his crimes. Even though it was all out now, all of it, I was shocked to see Ion's name there, written in black ink, followed by a list of his abuses.

"When I found out that the police were looking for me, I went to you, but you weren't ready to hear me. Later I drove to my house, to the house he had taken from me. I had to regain the deed to my house to show you and the police the proof that he had stolen my property. I knew that the combination of the deed and Volume 17 would reveal without question who he was and what he had done.

"There's a secret vault in the crypt, under the floor. My ancestors had secured it so that it could never be detected, and I knew that the property deed would still be there. I was sure Vadim had never found it. You have to know it's there and know how to gain access to it.

"I still had my old key and wasn't surprised when it fit the front door. You see? I didn't have to break in. I walked into my own house and went down to my family tomb. I wasn't shocked when I saw the weapons. I understand why he would collect such things.

"I went to the hidden vault and opened it. I found the deed was still in there.

"Here, you must use this," Anca said, handing me the journal. "You must do what is right."

10

I called the Hon. Mr. John Phelps, the man who looked just like an American ambassador should look, and told him I had evidence that Ion Vadim had committed Ana's murder.

The Ambassador was speechless, but listened to my story, and at the end of it said he would do whatever he could to help. I said I wanted him personally to take Anca and me to the police station to hand over the evidence to the police, and they must pick up Magda and Mihai on the way.

He was soon at my hotel, waiting in what looked like the same minivan that had taken me to Iași. He had picked up Magda and Mihai on the way to the hotel, and Dick Elbow was in the van, as well. Everyone watched Anca as she stepped into the minivan. Elbow apologized to me on the way to the police station. I accepted his apology, and handed him the unloaded pistol, removed bullets, and spent shell casing.

The driver who had taken me to Iași sat at the wheel. He glanced at me in his rearview, then promptly looked back at the road.

We went to the police station, and I told the whole sordid story, how and why Ana had been killed. I explained how Ion had been shot. I explained that I had been in love with Ion, not knowing who he was, thinking he was the person he presented himself to be. I told them Radu had to be released because he was innocent. I told them they had to arrest Ion because he was guilty.

The police chief, like all ambitious politicians, decided what to do based on that ambition and self-interest. He decided that it was in his best interest to ensure that the right person was tried for the crime and the innocent person let go. He said he would arrest the national hero and let the *Țigani* go free. But

Anca must remain.

A few days later Anca called me to say she had been released and told to return to her family home. She had been ordered not to leave the country.

Meanwhile, the Ambassador called me and said he had contacted several high-placed journalist friends and told them the story. His reporter friends were very excited about this scoop. When the story hit the Romanian press, Anca became a national hero. I turned on my hotel room TV, and there she was.

Anca called me again and related the current state of affairs. According to the news media, she had exposed the Romanian exemplar Ion Vadim as a sham, as the principal figure in Cozma's *Last Supper*. Anca was, the media said, "Romania Herself." The same man who had interviewed me on the cultural TV program was going to interview Anca. And the authorities decided not to pursue any charges against her.

Sitting in my hotel room listening to Anca, I noticed that my sinus infection was fading.

11

I could not wait to go home. I was tired of Romania, and wondered why I had decided to come in the first place. I got the earliest flight to LAX I could find. It would leave in two days. But before I left, I knew I must see Ion. I asked the Ambassador to help arrange it.

I sat by his bedside, looking curiously at this face I'd loved. The door was open and the police guards impassive.

"I feel like I should hate you, Ion, but I can't quite get there. Mostly I feel betrayed and deeply confused."

"It was a complicated world, Vita," Ion said. "I don't know if I can make you understand. I didn't start out that way, though. I want you to know that. I really was the 'crusading journalist,' as people like to call it. I really did write stories that exposed the Dictator's crimes. I was everything I told you I was, everything you read and heard about me, until several years before I met you.

"When they caught me and threw me in prison and kept me there and tortured me and starved me and I survived, they wanted me to work with them. They gave me a choice. To work with them or to work not at all, ever. I found out that I wasn't as brave as I thought I'd be, Vita. I wanted my life.

"And I discovered I had a taste for interrogation. I was good at it. I kept up the journalist persona as a cover. They approved of that, even encouraged it. The more outrageous comments I made about the Dictator, the more convincing. But my stories got less and less potent. People said it was because of my time in prison. They'd broken me down. But that wasn't it, really."

I hardly dared to look at him. Every thought that I'd slept with this man, fed him bites from my fork, laughed and joked with him, asked for his help, sunk into his arms, found comfort in his company made me feel like such a dupe, a sap, a fool. Heartbroken and stupid. Furious and stupid. Blind and stupid. Torn apart and stupid.

"So, was anything you told me the truth?"

"Of course. Everything about what I thought and felt and liked and disliked was all true. It was, is, all me. Even that I loved you."

Loved, I thought. Bullshit.

"Do you remember," I said, "when you mocked the Dictator for trying to make Vlad the Impaler a national hero? You wrote that Vlad had carried out such contemptible crimes against his own people that the Dictator was exposed as modern Romanian history's greatest hypocrite. You said that the *real* Dracula was the Dictator himself, posing as a champion while flouting everything decent and 'sucking the lifeblood from his own people.'" I looked at him. "Tell me, how are you different?"

Ion said nothing. He looked away.

"Just so you know, I could have shot you," I said. "It crossed my mind to take the gun from Anca's hand and shoot you myself, and I wouldn't have missed. I would have shot you right in the heart."

12

The Consulate picked up my hotel bill after all, and purchased my return flight. They also provided me with a car and driver to the airport.

I had to see Radu before I left, and there wasn't much time. When I talked to Dick Elbow about the car, I asked if the driver could wait a few minutes while I said goodbye to Radu, Magda, and Mihai on my way to the airport. Elbow said it was the least they could do.

The driver was once again the same man who had driven me to Iași and the police station. He looked at me in the rearview mirror again, but smiled this time.

Radu had called me as soon as he was released from prison. He said that the four of us could meet at the Lipscani café. Where it seemed so long ago I had met Ana and the others.

When I walked in, I saw that Radu was a changed young man, his spark diminished a little. But he rose quickly, laughed, and embraced me. He hugged me close for quite a long time, saying nothing. I think he was crying.

Everyone had a beer, looked at one another, and smiled wearily.

Radu said, "If it weren't for you, Vita, I'd still be in there. A dirty Gypsy stuck where he belongs. The dogs roam the streets begging for food, the same as the Gypsies, but the people love and feed the dogs! My people have lived in this country for centuries, but the *true* Romanians don't think I'm a Romanian. So I showed that I am a true Romanian by working to preserve the national heritage."

"What will you do now?" I meant the question to be for all of them. I knew that their lives would never be the same.

"If I'm going to have anything more to do with preserving the patrimony," Radu said, "it will be for a heritage that I can claim, too. I need to think about who I am and how I belong here." Magda brushed back Radu's dark hair from his forehead, and Radu grasped both of his friends' hands. "Magda and Mihai are helping me," he said.

I believed that with their help Radu would regain his once genial, lighthearted self.

"We will do what we can together," Mihai said. "We need to preserve some things, and there are other things that we don't need to preserve."

Radu said. "We're the Three Musketeers."

And everyone sat, sipping beer, remembering Ana. The Fourth Musketeer.

When I got up to leave, Magda said, "I wonder if you wish you had never come back here."

I looked at these very fine young people and said, "I'm glad I came back to Romania. I'm glad I met all of you. I won't forget you."

Radu said, "Vita is the Fourth Musketeer." And we all smiled.

Epilogue

After seventeen hours of flight, going back in time, I watched the lights of LA sprawl below. Millions of cars, streets, houses, people. From the air it is hard to imagine living in it—it seems more galaxy than city.

Lucha was waiting for me in the baggage area. After weeks of traveling, tragedy and heartbreak, her sweet, familiar face was like home to me. Lucha, my old friend, house- and cat-sitter.

"Vita, darling! We've all missed you, the cats and I."

Lucha was also one of *those* people. No matter what she'd been doing, Lucha, petite Lucha, always looked good. Her black hair smooth, her brown face unlined and seemingly unmade-up, though I knew it wasn't. It just looked that way, fresh and natural.

I embraced her, and she said, "I hope your jet lag isn't too bad."

"Strangely, I don't seem to have it."

Once in the car, Lucha asked how the "mission" went. Because of my regular travels abroad, it is a kind of private joke between us that I'm a spy.

"Nothing like I'd imagined," I said. "It didn't turn out to be what I had thought it would be."

Lucha thought for a moment, and said, "I'm sure it was nothing like the James Bond movies, where the hero comes out without a scar. A real spy's life must be exhausting."

I laughed. It felt good. I realized I hadn't laughed in some time.

"We missed that, too! Your laugh!"

I swung open the door and walked into my living room, a space uncluttered but warm, with just enough furniture, just enough color. A wall of bookcases. Black and white photos of friends and family and travels. The fireplace I'd often use at night now that winter was here. Auggie and Peanut stirred from their cat hammocks and greeted me with burbles and chirps. I picked them up and stroked them.

Sometimes you feel the forward and backward motion of time. I felt it then. The past I'd hoped to regain, a lie, the present, corrupted and violent, the past ever-present, but a different one, one I hadn't known existed. Tempted to berate myself—how could I have been so deceived?—instead I popped open a bottle of Napa Valley pinot, poured glasses for Lucha and myself, and handed one to Lucha.

It was a little chilly, so Lucha volunteered to start a fire in the hearth.

Out there, just beyond the bluff, was the vast Pacific. Ancient waters lapping the shore. I let my eyes gaze and unfocus. The lapping water I could almost hear. Ancient waves sifting ancient sands. If you're caught in it, it's deep, cold, and indifferent, but if you're at a distance, it's soothing, calm, and peaceful. Pacific means peaceful, after all.

"It seems presumptuous to take the tragedies of others and make them your own," I said, "but this is now a story in my life. A woman is dead. Friends are bereft, as are the family members I never met. Their lives will be significantly altered. The life of one will possibly change for good, while another has lost everything. And I lost love."

Lucha was listening to me.

"What do humans know of each other, really?" I petted my animals. "Cats are easy. They have few wants and needs. They have no secrets. But people, people are dangerous. Lives ocean-deep, histories."

Lucha sipped her wine, looked at me, and said, "Vita, tell me what happened."

"Okay. This is what happened.

"The leg between LAX and Paris was late, very late…."

ABOUT THE AUTHOR(S)

G. K. Holcomb is a pen name for Gary Edward Holcomb and Kimberly S. Holcomb. They are a writing couple, living in Athens, Ohio.

www.ingramcontent.com/pod-product-compliance
Lightning Source LLC
Chambersburg PA
CBHW061243170626
46809CB00007B/2802